Normal Enough

Allison —
I hope you enjoy
the book, and thank
you for your support.
Yvette Hatrak

Stories by
Yvette Hatrak

Cedar Hill Books   San Diego, CA 92104   2004

Copyright © 2004 by Yvette Hatrak
All rights reserved
Printed in the United States of America
First Edition

ISBN: 1-891812-34-3

Library of Congress Card Number: 2004103376

Grateful acknowledgement to *Cedar Hill Review, Bridport Fiction* and *Lummox Journal* in which several of these stories first appeared. I would like to thank Chris Noel, Maggie Jaffe and Thom Hofman for their invaluable assistance with this collection. I also wish to thank my family and friends for their encouragement and support. And to Vermont College, Vermont Studio Center and R&B Gallery for providing a creative and inspiring environment; without them, the creation of this book would not have been possible.

Distributed by   Small Press Distribution
                  1-800-869-7553
                  www.spdbooks.org

Cedar Hill Publications
San Diego, CA 92104
cedarhill_bks@hotmail.com
www.cedarhillbooks.org

for Karl

TABLE OF CONTENTS

FRESH-CUT GRASS 1

HAPPINESS IN SLAVERY 5

SWIM 13

ROOMMATE 21

ROLLING BLACKOUT 39

THE GIANT PANDAS 45

HABIT TRAIL 67

ADVICE FOR THE BRIDE ON HER WEDDING DAY 77

SHOPPING 83

NORMAL ENOUGH 99

LOVE LIKE PRIMATES 117

FRESH-CUT GRASS

I ignore the shitty cat you gave me on my 31st birthday. He no longer cries hungrily at the door. He just looks up and leaves the room when I come in. I'm not careful with the key as it hits the lock, the metal twisting itself inside the door. Christ, I would have dumped the dangling key chains we'd collected from Las Vegas, Catalina and Disney World, if I wanted to be careful when I came in.

I don't bother to shower when I get home, I don't use the Victoria Secret lotions you buy me in three's. I slip off my pink and black uniform from the Daily Grill, watching my name on a one-inch plastic tag butterfly to the ground. And for moments, what lingers in the air, in the room, in that horrible half-light at 4 a.m., is the smell of fried potatoes, spilt beer and a scent you didn't recognize a month ago—a scent that now, I imagine, you've grown strangely accustomed to.

I wonder, lying in bed next to you naked and not clean, how a man like you can sleep at night? How you can rest, your silhouette shaky on the wall you insisted we paint Sea Shell Green; how, with cologne that is distinctly not yours carelessly drifting in our room—how do you pretend to count sheep? And you sigh back at me as if to answer. I continue to ask these questions of you and count the stucco peaks on the ceiling, pretending they are mountains or stars that we wished upon when we were newlyweds.

"That one, Jane."

I roll over. Our backs are littered and wet with fresh-cut grass; your arm is extended and reaching for a star. "I wish frosted animal cookies wouldn't make you sick and your tongue wouldn't go stale after a whole bag."

"I wish Captain Crunch wouldn't tear up the roof of your mouth."
"I wish (we were kissing by now) coffee wasn't bad for you and—"
"And smoking was still cool."
"Yeah." (We were laughing by now).

In the mornings we don't talk over coffee and just two days ago I noticed you were drinking tea. "Did you get the paper?" I ask.

"It's on the porch." You finish the last of your tea and either the hot sip or the way you have to tilt the cup back makes your beautiful blue eyes small. "I thought you got it when you came in."

I close my eyes, I grab my dirty hair. I wish, I wish, I wish…

"No." I say.

… I didn't hate you for giving up caffeine and sleeping so soundly at night.

Of course, the cat circles my leg.

HAPPINESS IN SLAVERY

I've traced it all back to a donut with rainbow sprinkles. The bad haircut I got last week, the head cold I caught in October from going trick-or-treating with the twins in the rain. I never should have dressed up as a Genie mom and gone with my two Genie twins. The nail that went through the bottom of my foot last summer on the house boat in Tahoe, the flat tire on La Cienega and San Vicente, the two hot dogs I ate while waiting for the tow truck, the two pounds I gained from the hot dogs, the Thanksgiving dinner my husband and I are now shoving down the drain. I blame the donut.

Charlie is next to me in the kitchen but he is too pissed off to say anything—we're married long enough to know when not to say anything. As I continue to cut up the twenty-two-pound turkey into little disposal pieces that will fit down the drain, I remember an article I read in *Cosmopolitan* last month that said most married couples keep the passion in their marriage by fighting. I laugh to myself as I watch Charlie spoon-feed the drain mashed potatoes and yams—just like he used to feed the twins—and I am laughing because the last thing I want to do right now is fuck my husband no matter how many times he gives me a cold stare.

I think about the donut. I think about the donut in the donut shop in tenth grade. And I realize that there are moments in your life that are like the moments everyone talks about in death. Pivotal moments when your life flashes in front of you, events that change the course of your life forever. These moments happen in life all the time, but most people are too stoned or too mad or too busy fighting so they can justify fucking to ever realize that a moment like that had just passed. Standing in our newly remodeled kitchen with my husband in his traditional holiday corduroys is not one of these moments.

"I thought you were going to pay it."

"Do we really have to go through this again?" I'm not gentle with the turkey as I trim.

Charlie's mother laughs from the dining room; of course they think we are fine. Aunt Carol ordered the pizza, Grandma Smith said no pineapple or olives. My brother played with the twins, and Charlie's mother laughed—"I can't believe we're having pizza for Thanksgiving dinner." She's laughing still.

I suddenly hate what I am wearing and want to re-color my red hair. "You forgot to pay it."

"Why did you even ask me to do it?" He's growing older by the minute. "Just so I can fuck up again?"

I choose not to answer. Something our therapist taught me. I *choose* not to engage him. I de-cavitate stuffing, *choose* to ignore him and think of the donut instead.

Charlie forgot to pay the electric bill. I had asked him two days ago, I had given him the check, I had told him about the Carnacia Market on the corner that takes payments until 10 PM. Meanwhile, I thawed the turkey in the refrigerator for forty-eight hours. I peeled eight pounds of potatoes, I made the stuffing the night before, I managed to make two thanksgiving dresses for the twins. I got up at 4 a.m., bathed the turkey, stuck my hand—fingers first—all the way up inside it (I felt bad for the bird); I put him in the oven at 475; he cooked up nice and tan by 8 a.m. That's when Charlie remembered about the electric bill—about 8 a.m.

"Why are we paying our electric bills in person?"

"You don't even want me to answer that." I rip off a leg like it's a twig.

I had thought about that goddamn donut long before sending the turkey down the drain. I pretended not to care that Charlie would bring them home for Sara and Sierra, how the girls obsessed over the icing and the colorful rainbow sprinkles (Sara called them sparkles). I picked at a glazed or a bear claw with confidence, and I could pretend that the rainbow sprinkle donut didn't exist, I could pretend that the girls sucking on their fingers didn't exist, I could pretend that my husband, who had, for thirteen years, slept so heavily next to me in bed, did not exist. Today the donut is real.

"This is so typical." Charlie's shaking his head and the sink is getting full.

Green Beans, Pumpkin Pie, Homemade Cranberry Sauce.

"You were expecting something unusual? Something extravagant? I brought the cranberries to a boil for Chrissake. I jarred them. They're good. It's like jam."

"Here we go again." Charlie has the lumpy gravy in his hands.

I could've chosen the maple bar; they really were my favorites. My father had always brought one home special for me after he got back from business trips. Or even a chocolate glaze—can you really go wrong with a chocolate glaze? But I suppose I was enticed by the dense cake sitting all alone on the donut shop rack, white icing dripping down its sides. I suppose I thought those little colorful sprinkles actually made you happy. I suppose I thought it was cute, at sixteen, to say, "I'll take a rainbow-sprinkled, please."

That's why Tony noticed me, and I guess that's exactly what I'd intended by ordering the rainbow sprinkle: that someone would notice me.

"Only little kids order donuts with sprinkles."

I laughed in that horribly coy 90210 way and peeled a sprinkle off the top of the donut, placing the green fleck on the tip of my tongue, letting it sit there until it dissolved like a fine granule of sugar.

And that is, I imagine, when Tony thought about fucking me—while watching that tiny sprinkle disappear on my tongue—because before that moment we had just been friends. And that is, I imagine, how I ended up here shoving lukewarm poultry into a stainless steel drain. Before the moment with the sprinkle, I wasn't having sex—not even with Curtis who I'd been dating since the seventh grade and who was standing right next to me in the donut shop. Did Curtis know how complicated that green sprinkle was? "Sex complicates everything." That was another brilliant thing our therapist said.

"Why do you agree to do this every year, Anne?"

"It's just like you said, Charlie." I snap the wishbone under his nose and a splinter of bone sails across the room. "Just so you can fuck it up again." Of course I am left holding the short end.

Charlie is pathetic with turkey gravy on his hands, and for a moment, I feel sorry for him, as if he were wounded.

"I love being married to you."

"Fuck you."

I want to feed the garbage disposal his hand.

After that split second of melting sugar, I wasn't in love with Curtis anymore and I felt sorry for him, much like I did for Charlie just now, before imagining destroying his hand. It was all I could do to sit there between Curtis and Tony, two best friends, and eat my rainbow-sprinkled donut without throwing myself under the plastic table into Tony's crotch and asking Curtis, politely, to leave, sure that he wouldn't want to see me blowing his best friend.

I can't even remember the last time I did that to Charlie. What would *Cosmo* have to say about that? Needless Bickering and Trivial Name-Calling Bring Back Oral Sex.

I'm embarrassed thinking of the donut and Tony with fifteen relatives in the next room. I may even be blushing. But I look across at Charlie, who is bitter and cold, and it has nothing to do with the electric bill, and I don't give a shit.

"I'll take a twist."

"What?" Charlie questions me.

"Nothing."

I could've asked for a few donut holes or even a jelly, and just spent that afternoon sucking the jelly out of the hole, licking the inside until it was empty and flat instead of spending it with my head buried in Tony's lap. I wouldn't have told Curtis that I didn't want to be with him anymore. He was so destroyed; my mother said karma like that comes back on you. I wouldn't have had him hold me, hold me so tight it scared me—so tight I even let out a tiny yelp that made the dog bark outside, Curtis loosen his grip on my long red hair, and my mother knock on the door to be sure everything was O.K.

Charlie's mother is knocking at the door.

"Is everything O.K. in here?" Her famous laugh again.

"Everything's fine, Mom." We do this in unison. When she closes the door, we both let go of our smiles and continue to feed the stuffed drain.

It seems clearer now more than ever before what that rainbow-sprinkled donut was responsible for. More than just boyfriends, ex-boyfriends, my many one-night stands. The car wrecks, the night I ran out of gas and got picked up by a cop who liked my red dress and commented on my matching red shoes. I should've married the cop who liked my red dress. I should've gone to college when my mother died, she left me with all that cash. I shouldn't have bought the house in Santa Fe. No one can find work in Santa Fe. I should've told Charlie when he asked me after three months of knowing me, No, No, I won't marry you, I hardly even know you, I don't think I could ever love you, but instead I said yes, yes, yes. We went to the Bahamas for our honeymoon and Hawaii every year before Christmas. And he liked jazz and he taught me about sports and we both liked red wine, but I never loved him. And by that time, by the time I realized I wasn't the woman who was living in those red shoes, but rather the woman living in this dark house with the warm un-cooked turkey, it was too late to take back a bad decision, too late to ask for another life, let alone an apple fritter.

"Pizza's here."

"We're coming." Charlie looks over at me. "Let's go, we're on."

From the corner of my eye, I see him rinse the water around the sink and shove his hand down the drain, food swimming around in a little domestic lake. And maybe it's because he said "we're on", or maybe it's that I am too sad to pretend, or maybe it's the way he always hates the holidays, is allergic to pine trees, eats the green bean casserole I make with the cream of mushroom soup. Or maybe it's just because I can see his hand, how it fits nicely in the drain. And when I hear him say "on", before he can pull away, I reach for the switch. I flip it on and Charlie doesn't move, doesn't even try to pull away. Like he's frozen there, his hand tearing apart in the drain, his fingers crunching like the turkey bones, his blood much prettier than the cranberry puree. I can't let go of the switch and Charlie can't let go of the drain, and for a moment, a moment in which I am sure Charlie's little domestic life is flashing before his horrific green eyes, we forget the garbage disposal is electric, we forget that we have guests, we forget the pizza boy is waiting at the door for a tip; I am already wrapping Charlie's hand with a dishtowel, my brother is starting the car, his mother is holding the twins, someone has already called the hospital, someone is already saying they can't believe what I did. And I, I am sitting in the emergency room saying sorry, "I'm so sorry," eye-balling the plate of donuts next to the coffee machine with two of Charlie's disconnected fingers lying in a bag of ice in the palm of my hand.

I let go of the switch. In a moment, Charlie will remove his hand.

SWIM

I've been holding my breath through intersections for months now. Through tunnels on the 110 freeway, over the bridge down by the beach where you can't see the waves crashing in the distance but the smell of sea is all up in the air. Through the 91 Expressway, passing graveyards, train crossings, semi-truck weigh stations. The twin curves on Mullholland Drive, the two-way stop one block from my house, especially the two-way stop one block from my house. So poorly lit, so hard to see that there are just two stop signs not four. I start sucking in air before I get to the stop, maybe a few feet before. But as soon as I move my foot from pedal to pedal, I take the entire car in. Suck it up right through my mouth (I think my cheeks might even puff out), first the air then the windshield, the stereo, the cigarette lighter, I am full when I glide through the intersection. I close my eyes. I don't tell Bill about this, about closing my eyes. He is worried enough; he told the doctor I deliberately try to stop my breath.

"Are you superstitious?"
"I have a black cat."
Steve offers me a gingersnap.
"Thank you," I say.
Steve is who I see so Bill doesn't have to worry so much. I take the gingersnap.
"It's a child's game you play, Ellie." He is not a psychiatrist. I specifically asked for not-a-psychiatrist. "Holding your breath through tunnels and by graveyards." He is a priest with a degree in psychology. "That's a child's car game."
I ask him if I should call him Father Steve. He says he is neither Catholic, nor does he have children. "Calling me Father is a nice touch, but completely unnecessary." And besides, he says, I am not seeing you as a minister of the Lord, but as an observer of your mental health.
"I'm not playing a game, Steve."
I tell him that I too am neither Catholic nor am I insane, so it would probably be best for everyone if I called him just Steve. No doctor, no Father. Just Steve. How does one observe another's mental health, Steve?
"How is the cookie, Ellie?"
"It burns."

Just Steve is about to tell me I don't want his help.

"Ellie, if you don't want my—"

"Steve."

"Yes?" His eyes light up.

"The gingersnap." I am getting ready to leave. "It was a nice touch but completely unnecessary."

We both have the feeling that I won't be seeing him anymore.

When I am safely through the intersection two blocks from his house I let all the cookie-tainted air out of my mouth and the car fills with the smell of cinnamon and cloves. I buy a pine fresh air freshner for my car at the 7-11 along with a chocolate Yohoo and a bag of Red-Hots. It officially smells like Christmas in my car.

"What are you afraid of?"

When Bill asks me this I think he's talking in general. "Nothing," I say. It is like night in our bedroom and we lie on top of the covers, facing each other, the shades drawn tight, though it is just three in the afternoon.

"Other cars?"

I shake my head.

"An accident?"

I shake again.

"What then?"

"Has that lamp shade always been bent like that?"

"I don't know." I can feel how bad he wants to roll over and turn his back to me. "I guess."

"Funny how you can go without ever seeing something like that."

"Ellie." He grabs my hand.

"I mean it is really fucking bent."

Everyone is so concerned with this. As if it has been going on for years. As if no one holds their breath.

"What about those synchronized swimmers?" I tell my mother this over the phone. "I read they can hold their breath up to three minutes." She is finally back in Georgia now.

"There's a difference," she says.
"There is no difference."
"If they don't hold their breath they'll drown."
We both have the feeling that I will be hanging up now.

I look at the calendar just to be sure. Just to be sure I haven't been holding my breath for years. *November, December.* The cat calendar is posted to the fridge with the Carmel magnet from our trip up the coast last Spring. Two months, I say. It has only been two months.

The Carmel magnet has seagulls and seashells on it. I could never go back there with all those hairpin turns and blind bends. I would hyperventilate into a brown bag, I would pass out from a lack of oxygen and too much carbon monoxide, it would be a long time before Bill could revive me, people would stop on the side of the cliff with him, he would be embarrassed to tell them I had held my breath through Seventeen Mile Drive, he would be worried about brain damage by then. Going without air for that long, something inside me would be damaged for sure. Even the synchronized swimmers couldn't hold their breath for that long. Souvenirs like these are a good idea, I think. A memento from where you have been.

I run upstairs to tell Bill.

"Two months," I say. "It has only been two months."

Bill is busy fixing the bent lampshade.

Since October I have driven three thousand four hundred and eighty-four miles.

"Yeah," the mechanic says. "It's definitely time for an oil change."

Three thousand four hundred and eighty-four miles. Sixty miles an hour. One mile a minute. "That's why I brought it in," I say. As far as I can estimate I have held my breath for approximately one thousand three hundred and twenty seconds. "You better rotate the tires too," I say. Bill's mother said I have a death wish. "And check the antifreeze." That I am trying to punish myself. "Is it possible to get a wheel alignment here?"

We won't celebrate Christmas this year. How could we?

"How could they?" Stephanie, our neighbor says. "How could they even put one light up after everything that has happened to them?"

"Hi, Stephanie." People should always look behind them when they are standing in the produce aisle of their local grocery store talking to the neighbors about "what happened to them." "Good mangos?" I say.

"Huh?" It is pathetic to see her respond like this. She says it twice. Huh huh. Like a Christmas goose, all stuffed and ripe.

"The mangos in your hand." Everyone smiles and breathes. "Are they good this time of year?"

"Oh." As if she forgot she had a mango in her hand. Ha! "Oh, yes. Yes, quite good actually." She touches my hand. "Ellie, this is Martha Gilbert from across the street."

Me, Martha, and the Christmas goose exchange pleasantries, a Black Bean and Mango Salsa recipe, and then I tell them I have to go get a Christmas tree.

Good for you, they say.

Good for me, I say.

Of course, I never buy a Christmas tree.

"It's not your fault."

We are in the bedroom again.

"Stop doing this to yourself."

It is dark in the afternoon again.

"You can't do this to yourself."

I can't believe he is saying all this again.

"I need my wife." He pauses now. Always pauses here. "I miss *her* too, God how I miss *her*." The God part is new. "I need my wife back."

We would normally take a bath when it is cold outside.

"Say something, Goddammit."

"The God part is a nice touch, Bill." It is cold outside. "But completely unnecessary."

"Fuck you."

"Fuck you." And this is the only thing I can believe. "Fuck you too."

We continue like this until one of us leaves the room.

"Why don't you ever say her name?"

"What?" Bill has a drip of butter racing down his chin.

"You always say *her.*" I butter the asparagus right after I take off the steaks and turn off the grill. "Does it bother you to say her name?"

"I never thought about it." More butter is running. "I never thought about it that way." I suppose it will run for days.

"I took the car in for an oil change."

"I don't want you driving the car anymore. Not until you can explain to me this breathing thing."

"The asparagus was a little tough," I say. I am still watching the butter race. I point to a place on my chin. Bill wipes his mouth. "That's why I had to put so much butter on them."

"It's fine," he says.

"The steaks are underdone and the rolls are burnt."

"Everything is fine," he says again.

I cut into my soft steak. "There is still butter running down your chin."

One minute and thirty-four seconds. From the intersection on Monterey and Country Club I suck in, through the cemetery, the hospital and the 7-11 with the fudge squares by the register for 89 cents. I hold my breath for them. The fudge squares and their pretty- colored Chiklet friends. The car is humid from a big burst of warm breath, my lungs hurt and the windows seem to be covered with a liquidy film. The car is not moving and the engine has stopped

I hold my breath through a row of palm trees, alongside a bicycle lane, up and over the same curb that the ambulance hit the night I pulled her out of the tub. I didn't cry, I held my breath. I counted seconds through every intersection that was red. I got to sixty-two before the paramedic grabbed my hand and I said, "Do you know how you get a baby to hold its breath?" He grabbed my other hand and said, "You'll be okay, Ma'am." I didn't cry. I held my breath. "You blow in its face," I said.

She was blue and her blanket pink and the lines on the road yellow and the lights green and that is what made me think of the Chicklets in the 7-11, how completely colorful the entire night had been. How I held my breath, how I counted the freckles on the face of the two-year-old waiting for his father in the emergency room. Twenty-two. How accurate I was with my counting, how precise. How no one would ever know what it was like that night, those few seconds when she was no longer crying, no longer kicking, no longer splashing, no one would ever know the peace of that night.

And I refused to look at Bill when he said the Coke machine was out of Sprite, I refused to answer him because I was just sitting in the pediatrician's office on any other day, watching the mothers play with their toddlers, the crawlers tearing up pages of magazines, the infants and newborns sleeping peacefully in their car seats or in their mother's arms and I was just pacing, pacing back and forth like I did on any other day, waiting in the doctor's office, striking *her* a bit too hard between the shoulder blades to make that gas bubble that I had imagined after weeks of trying to dissipate was enormous, the size of a navel orange or pink grapefruit, a piece of produce inside *her* belly. I was not sitting in an emergency room still wet with bath water refusing Sprite. I was simply waiting for the pediatrician to call our name. For him to say, *it is okay. But she has been crying all night. I know. She's a colicky baby - it's just a tummy ache. I can't take her crying all the time. Where is your husband? He is at the university late. He has to get up early. Did I tell you she cries all night? Try to sleep when she sleeps.* It was just like any other day. And what a monster I was, a demon, to feel so free. And Bill would never be the same, and we would never be the same, and we would never do anything the same ever again, even going to the mall for ice cream would create pain. For every child in every stroller at every age would be unrelenting and, Sara with her blue, blue lips and compressed lungs, and sweet-smelling hair would be forever unforgiving for my not blowing in her face.

"The car will be okay." When Bill picks me up and the tow truck drives away even the Christmas lights on the street look dim. "Are you okay?"

As we go through the tunnel toward our house Bill's car, as if someone was able to make the night even darker, closes up and I hold my breath. I hold my breath as if it were tangible, as if it were a thing to hold too tight.

"Stop that," Bill says. "Just stop it."

And I think, what a funny thing for him to say.

ROOMMATE

They will tell you to get out more, to meet people, to pick up a hobby. The therapists, the friends, even new acquaintances will give you advice. Maybe pick up painting or cooking. "You've always loved to cook," they'll say. They will forget the time you burnt the crème brulee on Christmas day or the Easter they all got food poisoning from your deviled eggs. You'll forget too. You will say, "Cooking sounds great."

Or perhaps a pet. Get a dog or a cat. Someone might even suggest a gerbil—someone might even offer to throw in the cage. "It has a salt lick and everything." "Sounds great," you'll say.

And you need to get rid of the house, just move away. Too many memories in that house, too many rooms, just too much space. "It's such a big house," someone will say. Or at least get a roommate. To help out with the mortgage, to keep your mind off things. You'll say, "It's not such a big house." But then you'll say, "A roommate sounds great."

Carol is about thirty, thirty-two if I were to guess. She's tan and thin and spends too much time out in the sun, with too much coconut oil on her skin, lying by the pool, drifting lazily on the blue raft with the cup holder. I never use the pool much. I never even used it when Robert lived here. He loved to swim, to do laps. I called him "Fish."

I want to tell Carol to be careful with her skin—to worry about skin cancer—but we don't talk much, seldom disagree. The only time it's been anything other than polite is when I had to tell Carol that strands of her long brown hair, floating on ribbons of coconut lotion, get clogged in the pool drain.

"It gets sucked up into the filter," I said.

"Get a better filter," she said. She covered her eyes with her hand to avoid looking into the sun. She was lying on the raft. "I'll pay for half."

For three hundred and fifty dollars a month she gets one of the master suites in my five-bedroom house. It has a walk-in closet and an attached bathroom featuring a sunken tub. I hear her soaking in it when she gets home from work. She's a cocktail waitress at the new casino off the freeway.

We share the common space. I didn't even know that I had common space until I got a roommate. The area of commonality is fiction—people are otherwise, naturally, selfish and unpleasant within their confines. The living room and the kitchen are part of our common space. Carol doesn't cook much, though—she eats McDonald's Filet-O-Fish a few times a week for dinner and, before swimming in the morning, she'll eat vanilla yogurt. I should probably tell her deep-fried imitation seafood isn't healthy, but then again, it's just common space.

She's been here now for five months. She works graveyard: nine to five am. I get up early—about six—because I can't sleep. I hear her come in and, truthfully, it's nice to hear someone else in the house. I hear her keys in the lock and the shuffling of her feet (by this time they are usually bare, her black high heels off and in her hands). I hear her walk down the hallway into the bathroom. I hear the water run into the tub. When it's quiet she gets in and I get up. It's ideal, like clockwork. No complaints.

Today Carol comes into the common space when I'm eating lunch: half a tuna fish sandwich with a few slices of avocado and some Miracle Whip.

"Hi."

"Hi." I swallow. The dining room is off the still-incomplete kitchen. The tile doesn't meet the cabinetry, and the sink, never having been sealed with caulking, leaks. Robert left it this way. The space is huge, but when Carol comes in, it feels small and confining. "Going outside?"

She's in her lime-green bathing suit and she is tall—much taller than me—and, as she stands in front of the refrigerator, I can feel the invisible air cooling her skin.

"I have this friend." She's looking over the can of Ortega chilies and the diet soda. "He needs a place to stay for a few days. He lives on the street and needs a place to stay."

She's looking for the vanilla yogurt. I think I looked the other day. I think it had gone bad, maybe even turned a little green.

"His name is Fred." She turns around and looks at me, and for the first time since she entered the room, I'm aware that I'm sitting in this chair, at this table, finishing this tuna sandwich. Just minutes ago, with Carol standing by the fridge, I felt as if I were just a pair of eyes watching her—no body, no head.

"The vanilla yogurt went bad." I pick up my plate because I feel full and can't eat any more. I carry it to the sink. "Your friend can't stay. You only rent one room."

"He'll be staying in one of the other rooms." Carol is sliding out the door, putting on her sunglasses, and grabbing her blue raft. I can, through the sink window, see her outside. She is saying something to me through the glass; she is nodding and I'm acting like I understand.

"He can't stay here," I say again. I even shout this time.

She nods and floats away on her raft.

I turn on the water and drown the rest of the tuna.

"He can't stay here," I shout.

On Wednesday, when I go into the common space for a cup of coffee and a pen, Fred is in the hallway in a wheelchair with Carol standing over him. I left the pen there when reading today's paper. Sometimes the stories keep my mind off him.

"This is Elaina." Carol leans on the handles of the wheelchair. "She doesn't talk much and pretends to mind her own business. Her husband left her last year."

This is what I had told her.

"She thinks I'm too tan."

"No I don't."

"Whatever." Carol wheels Fred around. The entire time I've been standing here his face remains hauntingly expressionless. If I were asked, at this very moment, to describe Fred—even while staring at him—I wouldn't be able to tell you anything in particular. Anything other than 'he's in a wheelchair.'

"Hi," he says, "Nice place you got here."

"My husband built it." My voice is quiet and still.

"Cool." And then, suddenly, as if his voice controlled the muscles in his face, he smiles and I get a complete picture of him. All of him. Brown hair, dark eyes, good skin. If he were standing, I'd figure him about five-ten. There's something in his smile that tells me he's not paralyzed completely, not from the neck down. There's something natural and relaxed in the way he sits.

"Say hi," Carol says, moving Fred past me, barely hitting my big toe with the wheel of his chair. "This room has great light, huh?"

I watch them, the two of them, examining corners of my house, talking about the countertops and the couches. All that goes through my head is: you can't stay here, no matter how great your smile is. But when I open up my mouth, out comes, "What do you do for a living?"

"What do you mean, what does he do for a living? He's paralyzed."

"Just from here down," he says. He moves his hand slowly, skillfully, across his chest. His fingers look strong and callused. "I'm a beggar."

"Like on the street?" I say.

"Yeah, I've made some money there."

"That's your job?" I have my hands clasped along the arch of my back.

"Okay, so this is the common space," Carol says.

"I guess you could call it a job." Carol is maneuvering Fred around me and through the living room.

"What would you call it?" I ask.

"What's the big deal, Elaina?" Carol stops circling. "You don't even have a job."

"I'd call it a non-profit organization. A way for people to feel good about themselves." The rubber from his wheels is making dark marks on the tile.

"By giving their money to you?" I get on my hands and knees. "Well that's a novel idea."

"No it isn't." He's looking down at me. "It's been going on for years."

I look up at him.

"Like the Girl Scouts for instance," he says.

I lick my fingers and rub the marks on the tile. "What about the Girl Scouts?"

"Everyone knows those cookies taste like shit."

Carol is moving him again.

"You buy the cookies just to be nice." His voice gets louder to cover the distance. "At least I don't come to your door and ask for the money."

"You gotta be kidding me." I spit on the tile.

"All right," Fred laughs, "I admit—I like the Thin Mints."

At lunchtime we are all sitting at the pine table with the bamboo place mats, eating tomato soup and grilled cheese. Fred uses his right hand, which looks awkward—as if he is more comfortable using his left.

"Shouldn't you be asleep or something?" I ask Carol. By my calculations, she's been up for two days now. Forty-nine hours to be exact. In five months, this is the first meal we've ever had together, and I realize that this is the only reason we're still roommates.

"Fred got bit by a black widow last Saturday." Carol reaches over the table and pulls up his left arm. She jerks it so suddenly that his right arm, which had been holding the soupspoon, jumps. Soup splatters on the wall behind him. "Oops," she says. "Pollock." She laughs.

Fred turns his neck, just a bit, to look at the spots on the wall.

"Looks bad," I say.

There's a swollen red sore about the size of a nickel on the bottom of his hand, right where someone would normally fasten a watch or latch a bracelet. Everything around it, up to his elbow, is black and blue. The surrounding skin, like a snake's, is peeling away—the way Carol's did last month when she got burnt so badly from falling asleep in the sun.

"Pretty nasty," Fred says.

The house smelled like aloe vera for days. In the common space, her skin, sheer and thin like lace, floated over everything. Lace on the counter tops, the stereo, stuck to the TV screen. I picked up a thin two-inch strip off the kitchen floor and appreciated, for a moment, how beautiful its weightlessness floated to the ground. Then I sucked up all her loose skin through the vacuum hose.

"Just awful," I say again. "Must've hurt pretty bad."

"I can't believe you just said that," Carol says, dropping his hand.

"What?" And as I look over at him, I notice for the first time that he's wearing a hat. A European sort of hat. A beret, I think.

"He can't feel anything."

"I can feel some things."

"Shut up, Fred." Carol takes a deep breath and moves her soup bowl out of the way. "Let me explain this to you one more time." She tucks her hair behind both her ears. Whenever she does this, you can really see how green her eyes are. "He's paralyzed."

"He's eating soup."

"I have partial feeling in my arms." He holds up his right arm with the spoon. "See."

I look at him and wonder if he really felt it, the spider's teeth in his skin. Can partial-feeling really pick up something like that? How many days did the poison fester in there? How many days before he noticed it—just how close was he to death when he realized he wasn't okay? Wasn't quite right.

"Now, try to say something nice to Fred." Carol gets up and takes her bowl to the sink.

"You can't stay here."

"Try again."

I take a deep breath and look at his head. "I like your hat."

"Thank you." Fred smiles. "It's a beret."

Something is wrong in the middle of the night. I know something is wrong because I can't sleep, because I'm wide awake, because I've counted the shadows coming in through the window. I've made animal shapes on the ceiling. I've thought about getting up and getting some warm milk. Robert loved warm milk but I've always hated it. Found the smell repulsive, the idea a little crazy. And I start to think that I'm going a little crazy. A little nuts, I would say. I start to cry. Then I start to laugh when I realize how funny this all is. There's a guy in my house that I don't know, who begs on the street, who doesn't have a home. There's my roommate who's too tan and too thin and who lies on a raft all day, and I'm the one lying here in my bed thinking there's something wrong with me. I get up, I don't turn on the lights, I don't go to the bathroom; I walk into the kitchen and open up the fridge.

That's when he says, 'hi.'

"Jesus Christ." I jump and my head hits the inside of the fridge. "Shit."

"The vanilla yogurt is bad. I wouldn't eat it."

"I know," I say rubbing my head.

"Can't sleep?"

I close the door and it's dark again.

"No." I take a seat across from Fred in the living room. We sit there quietly for a while.

"How's your head?"

"Fine." I stop rubbing it, feeling guilty for making it a bigger deal than it is. "How's your hand?"

"Fine, I guess." He moves a few fingers around as if to test them.

Then some more of that uncomfortable silence that seems reserved for the common space.

"It's okay," Fred finally says. "I don't mind."

"Mind what?" The pain in my head is starting to disappear.

"That you don't want me here."

Fred is handsome in the dark. The moon is not full but the light through the window has made everything from the candlesticks on the wooden chest to the pillows on the couch—even Fred's profile, with his round nose and even lips—soft and blue.

"How do you know Carol?" I ask.

"From the casino."

In the shadow, he isn't in a wheelchair at all. He is sure and smart and ominous—intimidating even. Like your first college professor. I imagine that he must've really loved to play football. Quarterback, most likely. He was probably athletic in all things.

"You go to the casino?"

"I play poker there." And this exchange suddenly makes me feel like we're on our first date.

"Right." I say and pull my legs up in the chair and tuck them underneath me. "With all that money you make begging."

Fred laughs. "You have a real problem with that, don't you?" He has a nice laugh.

"It's not right."

"It's necessary."

"For you?"

"For you. You people need people like me." He looks down at his feet that are just square shadows on the foot supports of his chair. "Everyone wants a charity."

"Oh, so you're doing this for the betterment of society."

"That's right."

"Like you choose this."

"I do."

"You do this because you're stuck in that chair and you know people'll feel sorry for you." I shiver though there's no breeze in the air. "That's selfish and manipulative and I don't feel sorry for you."

"What do you do in this big house all day?"

"It's not so big." I put the tips of my fingers in my mouth.

"He must've been a real asshole to you."

I split my nails with my teeth

"To make you so bitter and afraid."

"Fuck you," I say matter-of-factly.

And for a minute, maybe just a few seconds, the night closes up the distance between us; it's maybe only a few inches, but the darkness takes over the room.

"I'm going to bed." And as I get up to leave the room, Fred just watches me walk away, still in his chair.

In the morning I get up late. I hear someone in the kitchen and I smell burnt coffee in the hallway. Fred's at the counter—his chin could rest on it—and he's buttering a piece of toast with his good hand and a fork. I realize how happy he looks, just buttering toast. "Where's Carol?"

"Out by the pool."

How content. How careful he is with the crumbs and how smoothly the butter spreads.

"Piece?" His eyes look back at me.

"No thanks."

Carol is on the raft. Her stomach is almost black and the smell of cocoa-butter lotion and burning skin reminds me of the coffee in the hallway.

"He can't stay." I am firm. I'm trying not to stare at her skin.

"It's only a few days." She runs her long fingers through the water, making tiny ripples and waves. "As soon as his arm is better he can work again."

"He begs!" I am stomping my feet and she's still making tiny, calm waves. "Would you stop calling it work!"

"It seems like work to me. All that smiling and pleasing and gratitude. Christ—it's my job without the free drinks." Her glasses are so big and so dark that even if she were looking toward me I wouldn't be able to see the expression on her face.

"He needs to leave."

"We're having dinner tonight, the three of us."

"He needs to leave today." I turn around and my sandal dives into a puddle of water, getting my toes and feet all wet. "Shit."

"You know, Elaina"—I hear her turn over on the raft, water splash, and then a deep breath—"You should really make a cheesecake for tonight. I think he would love that."

I take my sandal off and let it drip. I'm wishing I got a pet.

Outside the grocery store, with the ingredients to a Key lime-strawberry cheesecake in my cart, I run into Regina Basco.

"Elaina," she screams, actually running towards me.

"Regina," I say quietly. It's hot outside and the sun is making my eyes water.

"It's so—"emphasis on 'so'—"good to see you." She hugs me. I hug her back. We laugh.

Regina and her husband, Al, used to come over and barbecue with Robert and me every Wednesday. "I can't believe we still live on the same street and never see each other." She peers into my cart. "How's the roommate?"

"Fine," I say.

"And—" she gets serious—"how are you?" Emphasis on the 'you.'

"Fine," I say.

"You look fine."

"I feel fine."

Once we've established that everything is fine, we have nothing left to say.

How are you? How are you holding up? How are things? It's all code for the situation last spring. Good Friday, two days before Easter—all of it refers to this one-day last spring. And you let your friends have this: all this nonsense with words, all this fear of saying anything. It seems fair. In actuality, you are envious of their ability to disguise it all in pleasantries and idle conversation. You're envious of it, even if you haven't tossed out the rotten candy from last spring's Easter basket.

In the kitchen with the cheesecake I start cry.

On a good day, I'll cry for not feeling guilty about him. I'll look up at the clock, it'll be halfway through the day and I will realize I haven't had one thought of him—not one. This is what happens with the cheesecake.

I don't cry in the kitchen. I cry on the edge of the bathroom floor, right where the tile is connected to the carpet in the bedroom. So I leave the whipped cream cheese, the lime juice, and the eggs on the sink. There is no crying in the common space.

On the bathroom floor I force myself to think of him. I force myself into one of those infantile balls—back against the wall, legs pulled tight to the chest—and I go through the list of all the things I don't want to forget. He hated sweets, especially cake. He worked a lot (contractors usually do), we rarely had dinner together, and we never made love in bed. By the time Robert's head hit the pillow he was out. His breathing, deep and rich, would put me to sleep.

We made love in the shower after he shaved. He would wait for me, all that messing with my hair, all the toners and conditioners.

He loved it, though—my long, red hair. When we were done, when it was over—our knees sometimes shaking, sometimes not—he would get out of the shower and step toward the edge of the bedroom (where I like to cry), and I'd see him standing naked in the mirror while I'd finish rinsing out my hair. He would stand there dripping and naked and from then on it would be quiet in our house, peaceful, until one of us would say good night. "Good night," Robert would say. "I love you."

"I love you too."

The same routine almost every night.

Over the last few months, I have, while crying, pulled out the carpet's seam between the bedroom and bathroom. I've pulled out so much carpet that I have blisters on my fingers, have worn my nails down to their bed. I've stepped on carpet tacks; I've had them go right through the bottom of my feet. I've gotten horrible infections from them, but, being so numb and so tired, I don't notice the sores for days.

And on a good day, like today, I wash my face, take a few aspirin, and throw the pieces of carpet away. I don't stay in bed all day. I don't throw up in the sink. I finish the cheesecake.

Dinner is barbecued lobster with a great red wine. We're giddy and drunk by ten. We forget to eat the Key lime-strawberry cheesecake.

"I'm going to bed," Carol says. She leans over Fred, touches his forehead, and kisses him. "Good night," she says.

And something inside me makes me miss him—Fred—even though he is still sitting in the room, even though he's not going anywhere. My feeling is that I'm missing him.

When Carol's gone, Fred says she means well and asks if I want help with the dishes.

"No," I say, "I'll leave them till morning."

By the time we move into the living room, the candles have burnt so low that they're just beautiful orange and blue flames within puddles of colored wax. The room is darker than it was before. The last time we were in the common space.

"This is nice," Fred says, and his blue-gray eyes move around the room.

"Yeah, well—" I take a sip of my wine—"You know how 'we' people like to live."

Fred laughs. "I didn't mean you."

"You did mean me." And I smile. "I wasn't always this way." The breeze coming through the small crack in the courtyard window hisses and makes its way over us in the dark. "When you said I was bitter and afraid—well, I just wanted you to know, I wasn't always this way."

"I know that." His voice is assuring and warm. "Believe it or not," he pauses, "I haven't always been this way." A few of his fingers point down to the chair. "Bad things happen and people change."

He's dressed well tonight. In a polo shirt Carol bought him at the casino gift shop and a pair of blue slacks.

"What happened to you?" I am startled at the tightness in my throat, the shape of the words in my mouth.

"I slammed my car into a tree."

"On purpose?"

"Yeah." He looks up at me. "Eighty-five miles an hour of purpose to be exact."

And we both laugh (though it's not his nice laugh). We know it's not funny.

"How long ago?" I hold onto the glass of wine and place it below my lips, like a microphone.

"Seventeen years." And when he says this, I realize how young he looks. That he's probably only in his late thirties, that this happened to him at a young age. And I think: how devastating to want to slam your car into a tree at sixteen or seventeen.

"After the tree," he smiles at me, "people wanted to do things for me. Not just family—though there weren't a lot of them around. Complete strangers wanted to do things." His smile shows a sliver of teeth, a glowing half-moon in the dark room. "Not everyone stops. But the few who do, they roll down their window and hand me a dollar or a five and I smile and they smile and I know they'll be talking about it, this act of gratitude, this unselfish thing they did in their otherwise selfish day, they'll be talking about it all the way to work, in the lunch room, after dinner over drinks. They'll go home and share it with their kids and everyone will say, 'how great' and 'how kind' and they'll feel so good about themselves, so humane." He finally takes a breath and his chest rises high, almost to his chin. "And that's what I do for them."

When he stops I'm glad we're in the dark. I'm thankful for the night and the moon's unwillingness to be bright. "Why wouldn't everyone stop?"

"Because most people realize it only changes them. Not me." He stares down at the wine cupped in between his legs and his smile fades. "When did he leave?" He looks up at me.

"It'll be a year in April," I say, and my throat strangles on the words again.

"Did he hit you?"

I shake my head and press the rim of my glass harder against my mouth. It makes a small squeak across my lips.

"Cheat on you?"

My lips squeak again. "He loved me. He was just always busy."

"Carol told me he was a contractor."

"He built this house."

"I like this house." And somewhere between the hissing wind, the wine glass on my lips, and the sound of Fred's chair in this room—somewhere between still and alive—I am telling him everything. I am telling him all about Robert and me and the three years we were married. I am telling him about the trip to Disneyland where we paid for the family behind us to get in.

"He was real generous that way," I say.

And I tell him smaller things, intimate things, things I haven't told anyone, things I haven't thought of in over a year. Like the way he would hold onto the edge of my ear when we would drive, his elbow resting on my shoulder. He'd gently rub his finger and thumb over the edge of my ear, like it was something precious and valuable, something to be careful of. Or the way he made blueberry pancakes: dropping the blueberries one by one on the grill before pouring the batter over them.

"He said it toasted the berries and that they tasted better that way."

"I love blueberry pancakes."

"Me too," I say.

Then I'm telling him about the nights he couldn't sleep, when he had so many things on his mind that he didn't want me to worry about. Then I am telling him about the tile and the edge of the carpet and making love in the shower.

"I have to put a lot of stuff in my hair."

Then I am telling him what I haven't told anyone in almost a year.

"And then I said, I love you too."

"And that was it," Fred says.

"That was it," I say. "Good night, and I love you."

While Fred is wondering if he should ask me all the things he wants to know, all the horrific details everyone wants to know, I watch the very last candle flame drown in a pool of wax.

"Go ahead," I say.

"I can't."

We both have our eyes focused on the smoke and cooling wax.

"After they take the body away, you have to pick up the pieces of brain yourself." I make my lips squeak one last time on the edge of the glass. "I still can't get that stain out."

When I wake up in the morning, my head hurts and my eyes are swollen a bit. I sit up straight and remember what happened between Fred and me. And when I start to panic, start to feel guilty for sharing so much with him, I look at the edge of that carpet and start to feel sick, start to feel mad. And although that's what they all said would happen—how angry I might get at Robert, how getting mad doesn't mean I didn't love him—this is the first time I really feel pissed. I could throw up on that carpet, I could tear it to shreds, I could never use this bathroom again; instead I get up and put on my robe.

In the kitchen I pour myself some coffee, and I hear Carol come in. She's still in her uniform. She's still smoking a cigarette.

"Sorry," she says and throws it out the door.

"Coffee?" I say.

"No," she says.

"How was work?" Her uniform isn't as small and revealing as I had imagined.

"Okay." She throws her shoes down. "What's going on here?"

"Nothing." I watch her go to the fridge, open it. She almost puts her whole body in.

"You're talking to me, you're offering me coffee." She's looking for the vanilla yogurt again. "What's going on here?"

"It went bad," I say, and pour more cream into my coffee. I don't stir—I watch it sink and rise and eventually dissipate. "I threw it out. The vanilla yogurt."

"Fred's gone." She picks up an apple instead. "Spider bite all better, he's back to work. Aren't you relieved? Now things can go back to the way they were." She takes an enormous bite out of the apple—almost half the apple really. "Avoiding each other in this big place."

"Where?"

"What do you mean where?" Her mouth is so full; with her skin so tight and tan, I hope it doesn't explode. I hope her skin has enough moisture to expand.

"He must have a place. You know, like a regular spot."

"Why do you care? You don't even like him."

I grab my cup and walk past her. "I don't care." I throw the coffee and cream down the sink. "If I cared I would tell you that you have terrible skin."

"Thanks," Carol says.

"Don't mention it," I say.

I hear the skin on the apple break as I walk away.

I find him on the corner of Indian Canyon and Ramon, very close to the casino. Next to a freeway on-ramp and a drive-thru Wendy's. He's in the same clothes he was in yesterday, and, in this context, from this distance, he looks alone and afraid—not as confident and handsome as he did in the common space.

I sit in my car at the light, just watching him. A few people roll down their windows and give him money; he is polite, he says thank you.

The sign in his lap says, "God bless you. Have a nice day." He's wearing his purple beret.

I'm going to get out of my car and go over and ask him. Get up and walk through the wind, the sand; dodge a few tumbleweeds; and ask him. Ask him to move in, to be my roommate. Tell him I'm going to help him. Find him a job—a real job—so he doesn't have to beg. So he can get off the streets, so we can drink red wine and eat cheesecake. So we can talk in the dark. I'm going to tell Carol she has to leave.

But like most people, when the light turns green, I just drive away.

ROLLING BLACKOUT

Carla's husband is going to die on a Sunday. Because he has stage four Non-Hodgkinson Lymphoma. Because it came to her in a dream—an angel telling her the exact day of the week. "Any particular Sunday?" I ask.

"He didn't say."

"The angel was a he?"

"The angel was Ed Harris."

Because she's always been an Ed Harris fan (loved him best in *The Abyss*); because he's going bald like Bob (the chemo taking all Bob's hair); because in that one movie when NASA loses a bunch of guys in space ("*Apollo 13?*" I say, "Yeah," she says. "The one with Tom Hanks."), Ed Harris says, in vest and tie, "I've never lost a man on my watch and I'm not going to start now"—that's the same thing the oncologist told her three weeks ago when the cancer moved to Bob's neck and brain.

"The doctor really said that?" I ask.

"Well, not in so many words, and with much less drama than Ed Harris."

Bob's been dying for six years now. For each of the six years he's been dying, Carla's lost 25 pounds. Which is okay considering she was 320 pounds before he got cancer. And she always says *the cancer,* which can mean either Bob's deteriorating health or her miraculous weight loss. Sometimes it's hard to be sure when she says things like, "before *the cancer* I never used to eat like this" and "after *the cancer* I started going to the gym." She's an inspirational icon of sorts at the Oasis gym—she's even met Richard Simmons. "What was it like?" I asked. "I was fat and he cried," she said.

She talks about Bob as if he isn't dying, as if he still has years to live. Sometimes she will complain about him, like all wives complain—like I complain—"He doesn't tell me he loves me enough, and I don't think he's ever thanked me for a single meal I've cooked." Even though we laugh at this, like most wives do, I feel bad when I finish chuckling. Not for sick Bob as the object of complaint, but for

Carla knowing that she won't have him to complain about much longer. Maybe, I figure, she's just getting all the complaining in while she still can.

Today at the gym, she tells me that in the twenty-two years of marriage he's never told her that she looks good.

"Not even since you lost all that weight?"

"Especially since I've lost all this weight." She's on the treadmill again. "He thinks I'm just getting ready to date again."

And then all the electricity goes out. I land hard on the Stairmaster step and Carla almost falls right off the treadmill. We should be accustomed to this striking kind of halt by now.

"Not again," she says, and we get off the machines, go sit in the aerobic room, and wait in the dark with our water bottles and gym towels.

Our grids are empty. That's what the newscasters and local papers say, at least. 120 degrees in the desert; 150,000 residential air conditioners; not to mention condos, hotels and golf course clubhouses. Then, of course, there's the brand-new casino off the San Bernardino freeway. *We are in a constant state of emergency.*

"'Rolling blackouts' is just a technical term Edison came up with for 'We-didn't- pay-our-electrical-bill.'" Carla wipes a thin layer of sweat from her forehead and we both laugh.

"Yeah, how come they don't get a notice that says pay by 5PM?"

And we laugh again.

Because this is funny, and because there are just some things you don't talk about in the dark—death being one of them. And no matter how much we pretend (and we both pretend), when we talk about Bob in the dark, we can't pretend he isn't dying. We can't pretend he isn't as sick as Ed Harris said. She can't pretend that she's not angry with him for all this sick and dying business, and I can't pretend that I'm not her friend who's having the affair, the one who's cheating on a husband whose cells are perfectly patterned, not cancerous, not relentlessly attaching themselves to spine and bone marrow. And, if this is the case in the dark, then I can't also pretend that this isn't fucked up or self-centered—sitting in here with my soon-to-be-widowed friend thinking about my affair and the energy crisis.

"Annette, I don't think I can take much more."

I can't see her face but she sounds sad.

"Don't worry," I say, putting a hand on her lap. "It's just another blackout."

And we wait quietly for the lights to come back on. As soon as they do, Bob is not so sick again.

In the evening, when I get home from the gym, all the lights in the house are off except for the one in the room he—Cal—is in. Cal is conservative this way. He cares about our depleting grid. Just like he cares for stray cats. He's even set up recycling bins in the kitchen next to the fridge.

These are the moments I will miss: when he hasn't noticed that I've come in, when he doesn't realize I'm looking at him bathed in computer-generated light. It makes his face white and electric, like the moon's surface at night. This is when I start to mourn him, really grieve for him. Forget about the distance ten years of marriage can put between a couple with no kids.

I imagine myself talking about him as if he were the one dying, and not Bob. Not Carla losing her husband, but me. What if Cal were dead? How would I tell all my friends about the recycling bins? How would I tell them about the way he'd call me 'love', and 'angel'—never my real name, rather names given. How would I tell them about the pigeons and doves that slam into our windows on clear spring days, with the sky so blue and the clouds white-white? I'll tell my friends—my parents, too—how he would hold these fallen birds, how he would scoop them up, their tiny necks broken, their heads resting on the flesh of his thumb as if sleeping on a pillow. He would make little bird graves and bury each one of them. How endearing a backyard full of dead birds would be if stage four Non-Hodgkinson's Lymphoma were happening him. Wouldn't we all just sit around and cry for the birds and for Cal and for my missing him?

"Hey," Cal says, "I didn't see you standing there."

And I go over to him and hug him, hold him there. And he lets me sit on his lap as if nothing strange just occurred. Nothing unusual at all.

And soon, after we kiss, he'll ask me how's Carla. "How's Bob's health?" I will forget to tell him her dream about Sundays, or what the doctor said: how a transplant might be their only hope but the hopes of a bone marrow transplant are slim. Instead we talk about dinner, where we should eat, what we will have. And when I tell him I have to shower still, he leaves the room and turns off the light. I check my e-mail in the dark bedroom, the adjoining bathroom's shower steam creeping in and encircling my head. I am sick. My stomach is tight and knotted as I wait for the messages to appear onscreen.

And when I find one from you, I'm sicker still. I pretend for a moment that you're not telling me when we'll meet. What day? What time? Where? The way Cal and I discuss dinner plans: "I feel like sushi." "Sushi closes at nine. How 'bout Mexican?" In this moment, you're not telling me you miss me, and Carla's husband is not sick—he's still healthy and hiking in Montana where they have a cabin on the lake—and she's still over 300 pounds, and birds aren't slamming into windows, and I am not cheating on a man whose white blood cell count is an extravagant seven thousand nine hundred ninety-nine.

You want to meet me on a Sunday as if you've heard.

Before I can hit *reply to sender* another rolling blackout occurs.

THE GIANT PANDAS

The Zodiac Casino is off the 10 freeway. It doesn't have a midnight buffet, or a progressive jackpot; there are no theme parks for the kids. This isn't Caesar's Palace. This isn't the Bellagio with its 2.5 million-dollar lobby entrance (you've all heard of the lobby entrance). This is Morongo, by the dinosaurs, off the 10 (think hard, you've seen the dinosaurs). This is not the City of Sin.

So let me make one thing perfectly clear. I'm not the girl you think I am. I'm not cocktailing the blackjack tables, hoping to be discovered and put on some shitty soap opera like *Santana* or *Hunter Falls*. I hate soap operas. I can't act. I can't even tell a joke without fucking up the punch line. *And that's why God made Adam.* See? Nobody laughs.

I serve drinks from eight till two a.m. I wear short skirts, make macaroni and cheese and serve it to my beer-drinking boyfriend, Steve. I see my mom on Sundays. I buy bridal magazines. I don't own a dog. I'm not the girl who'll be rescued in the end.

So if you're terribly bored by now, let me assure you I've been bored for days—for years, really—but I get up in the morning and rub the sleep from my eyes. I sip hot coffee, eat toast, think about fixing the broken patio chair. And I ask Steve again, while he's asleep, while he's still full of booze: what about us? What about forever? What about Christmas dinner from Pavilion's with two kids? But Steve never answers, and the coffee is always salty, the toast always burnt, and I have to tell myself again and again that this is just one broken patio chair.

"This is just the hand you hold, the cards you've been dealt," Victor says, the pit boss from eight to two. "Face it, Ginger—sometimes the ante is already in."

The employee handbook at the Zodiac Casino is forty-two pages long. You read it, you sign it, you live it. You pay attention to the important stuff and hope the fine print applies to somebody else. Steve laughs and says, "Just like life." He's drunk again.

REPORTING FOR YOUR SHIFT
All casino employees will enter and exit the building from the main rear door with access to parking lot A-4. Personal belongings will be inspected by security at both the start and close of your shift.

"Why won't he fuck her?" Linda is talking about the panda bears at the L.A. Zoo. They've been cooped up for days together. Circling each other, creating territory and marking space in the breeding pen.

"Maybe she won't fuck him," Bill says.

"Viagra could save them." Linda's a showgirl. It's 7:55 pm.

Bill checks bags. I hand him mine.

"Maybe he knows." He's a good checker. "Just maybe he knows." He digs deep.

"Knows what?" I ask.

"Knows that this is the bitch that'll cut off his hand." Bill's been at this for twelve years. "Ginger" (I'm not even going to answer you if you ask me if this is my real name) "did I ever tell you about the shift when I found two fingers in a showgirl's bag?"

"Always a showgirl," Linda says.

"No," I say, though in two years, I've heard Bill tell this story sixteen times. It's the universal story for avoiding commitment. Someone always ends up with someone else's hand.

"Chopped off her husband's fingers and just threw them in her bag." Here comes the connection. "Maybe pandas are just like people and aren't meant to be caged up together."

"I don't think they let the panda bears have sharp objects, Bill."

"Maybe they need some good porn." Linda's on her way to the locker room.

"Ginger"—Bill smiles and talks real low as he hands me back my bag—"are you sure I haven't told you that story before?"

"Never," I say. Seventeen times, to be exact.

UNIFORM POLICY AND PROCEDURE
Employees must leave their uniforms in the locker rooms at the end of each shift. Uniforms will be cleaned and returned to your locker before your next shift. There are cameras in each of the four employee locker rooms.

"How do they know they aren't doing it?" My mom is setting the table.

"You can say 'sex,' Mom," Susan yells from the kitchen.

This is Sunday night dinner with my mom and sister. The Waltonesque quality of the whole thing makes me sick.

"How do they know they aren't having sex?"

"They have cameras on them." I'm picking at a patch of lint. I can't wear black jeans without attracting lint.

"They watch them?" She sets methodically. Knife, fork, spoon.

"They have to."

"That's degrading." Susan enters with her meat loaf as if presenting a roasted pig. "Ta-Da!" Sunday night dinners at Mom's were her idea. Susan's husband, Al, is having an affair.

"Everything looks lovely, dear." Knife, fork, spoon.

Gag. Oh, look here, another piece of lint.

Susan is upset. She cooks when she's upset.

"Degrading," she says again, "to put a camera on them."

Al is at the Zodiac almost every night. He told four cocktail waitresses, one bartender, and twelve showgirls that Susan doesn't like to give head. He gets loud when there's not enough vodka in the orange juice, enough twenty-ones in blackjack, enough showgirls with big tits.

As we eat the garlic-mashed potatoes, the meat loaf, the fried chicken, the green beans and mushrooms with basil croutons, the homemade gravy, the zucchini nut bread, I'll forget to tell Susan it doesn't take a camera for someone to degrade you.

"Pass the potatoes, please." I'll forget to notice how much Al makes her cook.

Unlike the panda bears, I don't mind the cameras in the locker room. In fact, I might even like them. I think of what underwear I might wear, what manager will be watching the tape, whether or not he'll like my satin black g-strings that say "Poison Partied Here" or the cotton ones with mulberry flowers. Whether or not he'll think of them when he makes love to his wife, or when he jacks off in the shower. Either way, I think of them. The cameras and the men.

"I like your pink ones," Steve says. "You look like a school girl in them." I let a comment like this go; the complications of taking it seriously are often more than I can deal with before my shift.

THE GIANT PANDAS

I usually choose something red. Susan says red is sexy. "Men love red." I want to ask Susan if Al loves red. At the blackjack table, 2 a.m., with his hand far up a blonde's ass, I don't think he cared too much that she wasn't wearing a stitch of red.

Naturally, Susan's garlic-mashed potatoes have become quite superb.

HOURS OF OPERATION
The Zodiac is open 365 days a year, 24 hours a day.

The Zodiac closed once last Christmas—four a.m. on Christmas Eve till four p.m. Christmas day. Twelve hours. When I got to work on the twenty-fifth, the off-ramp was backed up for two miles, and the line at the entrance (guarded by security because locks were never installed on the Zodiac's revolving doors) reached the McDonald's across the street.

"Fucking four o'clock on Christmas day," I said.

I waited at the back door for Bill, disappointed that the small box from Steve was the key to my new luggage set and not an engagement ring. I stared at my naked finger and ate my Fish Filet.

Yesterday they put a panda-cam on the web: www.pandacam.com. You can watch what they're doing twenty-four hours a day. I figure the real whack-jobs log on hoping to see a little panda porn. I log on at night when Steve is heavy and passed out. I watch the pandas ignore each other. As if the other one isn't even there. She's smaller than him by nature; she instinctively knows to move right when he moves left. This game of chess can go on until six a.m., until I crawl into bed, until I curl up next to Steve, until he curls the other way.

Steve says when the pandas finally fuck, they should put it on pay-per-view. "I'd pay," he says.

JOB DESCRIPTION
Your position at the Zodiac Casino will be clearly defined by your immediate supervisor. Your duties will be outlined in writing and signed by both employee and employer.

"It's more than passing out a few drinks and collecting some fucking chips." Victor always talks to me this way. "You have to flirt with them, Ginger."

If you're picturing Victor as your typical Italian pit boss, let me again remind you that this is Morongo, not the City of Sin. The man you're picturing would terrify Victor.

"Be nice to them." However, his mouth *is* full, he *is* fat and he *is* eating veal Parmesan. Still.

"He's my brother-in-law, for Chrissake." My high heels are never hard to stand in, never hurt my feet—not even when I work a double. Only when I talk to Victor. Only when I watch him eat.

"Ginger." He uses a sharp knife, and he's a fast cutter. "I don't give a shit if he's the fuckin' Pope." He leans forward and grabs the inside of my thigh. The knife is tucked just far enough back in his hand to miss my skin. "You smile when a customer grabs your ass." He pinches my thigh and lets go. "You smile big!"

I tell Steve I bang into a lot of things when he asks about the thumbprint on my thigh.

"You look like a whore."

"I'm not a whore."

"Who grabbed the inside of your thigh?"

I won't tell him it was Victor because, when Victor asks about the bruises on my eye or on the inside of my arm, I won't tell him it's Steve.

"I'm leaving."

"Leave." The bride magazines say communication is the key.

I bang into things at least twice a week. My mother tells me to eat more tomatoes. "You bruise too easily. You need more vitamin K." Susan makes an excellent stuffed tomato.

Tonight, when Steve comes back from the casino after a few drinks, when he's good and drunk at two a.m., we'll sleep—he'll forget he called me a whore, and I'll forget to tell him the pandas are still sleeping at opposite ends of their cage. He'll climb on top of me, sloppily and heavily. He'll fuck me and ask, "Do you love me? Do you really love me?"

But I'll pretend that I'm asleep.

EMPLOYEE RELATIONS

On Fridays, Linda and I stay late in the lounge. We listen to Frieda sing "Fifty Ways to Leave Your Lover." Linda buys me a beer and smokes two of my cigarettes. Victor buys Frieda a shot of whiskey and tells her she has the sweetest voice in the Morongo Basin. Frieda is tone-deaf, but she swallows. These are the only qualifications for a lounge singer at the Zodiac.

I hand Linda a cigarette. She's slicing lemons and limes for the bar.

"I'm *so* glad I quit smoking," she says, lighting the end of the cigarette. She cuts the limes in quarters, then scores them down the middle. "Fuck." She barely nicks her finger and holds up her hand. "Workman's Comp."

I laugh. She laughs. And we inhale.

Linda has been at the casino for years. With those strong calves and thick wrinkles beneath her eyes, she tells everyone that only the dancing has kept her alive.

"Still buying those bride magazines?" she asks.

"Yep. I love the ads with the couples pretending to be in love." I grab a lemon and make an incision.

"Are they also pretending to be faithful and sober too?" She laughs. Linda has been married eight times.

"You bet." I like the bridesmaid dresses the best.

"Steve still hasn't asked?"

"I don't want him to ask." I can cut ten lemons while Linda smokes one cigarette. I've timed it.

"Yes, you do." She sucks in deeply when she smokes. "We all do."

I've tried on two hundred wedding gowns, tasted eighteen pieces of cake, heard over a dozen string quartets. All in my mind, all while sitting here on Friday nights with Linda, Frieda, my beer, and slices upon slices of lemons and limes. And each time, each night, I'm completely aware of how beautiful it all is—how perfect it all looks on glossy pages with paid models sipping white wine from frosted flutes. "I told you I just like the ads." I'm aware that the flutes are plastic and the white wine is apple cider.

"I just thought you would have given up on that by now."

Linda would never wear an emperor-waist gown. "How's your hand?" Steve would never drink apple cider.

"Look," Linda points at the TV. "It's on the news."

"He still hasn't fucked her yet?"

"Ginger"—Linda lights her second cigarette—"It's really not that bad." And because she isn't looking at me when she says this, I assume she's talking about the cut on her hand.

I met Steve at the casino. He came in with his brother one night, dirty and salty from a long day at work.

"Scotch."

"JB?"

"Chivas."

I was twenty-eight, cocktailing from eight to two a.m. It was enough that he ordered the best scotch we had.

Steve asked me that night while lying in bed, "How'd you end up here?"

"What do you mean here?"

"Here." He rolled over on his side to face me and the intimacy between us then—the feeling after fucking a complete stranger—was the closest I would ever feel to him. "I mean, what else did you want to do with your life?"

"What if I told you I always dreamed about being a cocktail waitress?"

He laughed. "I'd laugh."

"What's so wrong with here? Here is just geography." I pretended not to care how much I loved it when he touched my hair.

Steve sighed and looked around. "It's hot in here." It was my trailer but he looked familiar with all its corners. The wood siding I painted white, the windows I tinted so I could sleep in till at least ten. The homemade curtains, the framed photographs. "Didn't you ever want more than this?"

I started to cry.

"What's wrong?"

"I promised myself I'd make you leave if you asked me that again."

BENEFITS AND INSURANCE

Section 23c: Any cosmetic surgery that will ultimately benefit you in your position at the Zodiac Casino will be covered under your insurance policy and will require a five-dollar co-pay.

I got a boob job last week. Steve, of course, thinks they look great, though he can't touch them yet. You'd be surprised at how little really goes into enlarging your breasts.

"But no one has any rights on Indian land. They have their own law there. Their own police. They have their own police cars." We're having the Indian law argument again.

"Calm down, Susan." I help with the salad. There's mango all over my hands. "No one has ever seen their police cars. You don't even know if they exist."

They exist. Casino land is Indian land; Indian land is sovereign land. Trail of Tears, Running Bull—tax exemption and cool police cars somehow make up for all of this.

"Can we change the subject, please?" This is a favorite non-confrontational line for 'you don't know what the fuck you're talking about' in my family.

"I made a cake last week." I think Al's living in the Comfort Inn. "Triple layer, fudge filling, raspberry ganache and mocha frosting." I think Tina, the lead showgirl, has a good time with him.

"I'm sorry I missed it. I had a doctor's appointment."

"A girl was raped out there last Saturday." Now my mother starts in.

"I heard."

"They'll never prosecute them." Susan drizzles the salad with an aged balsamic vinaigrette.

"Because they have their own police cars. I know." I move my mango hands to avoid the gourmet drizzle. "Can we change the subject again?"

Susan presents the ham with a smile.

"Ginger"—my mother takes a thick piece—"are those your real tits?"

My mother is afraid. She's afraid of many things, but currently, asking me if these are my real tits, she's afraid that the casino is corrupt, that I'll get a boob job, that Steve will never marry me and that the next step up from a cocktail waitress is a showgirl and then a stripper. (They are.) (I have.) (He won't.) (It is.)

"No." I quickly take a biscuit.

"How can you afford those?" Susan is slicing the ham way too thick.

"I have great insurance."

"Aren't they cosmetic?"

"No"—I grab the butter—"just a five-dollar co-pay."

"Susan," my mother shouts. "Stop slicing it that way."

VACATION TIME
After a three-month probationary period, each employee will receive one-week paid vacation. No employee will be allowed vacation time October through May, holidays or weekends.

I take the time off work when I hear. I take the two-hour drive to L.A., on the 10, the 210, the 5. It's never a nice drive on the 5.

I sit on the sticky bench and eat a Safari Cone with chocolate ice cream. I ignore the pain from my fake tits. I watch the kids buy the waxed figurines—they put their quarters in the machine, and thirty seconds later, get back a bright orange panda bear.

"Seventeen stitches." That's what Linda heard the news say. He got her on the side of the face when she tried to go over to his side of the cage.

The wax figurines present the bears in a choice of three colors: orange, yellow, or lime green. Both bears wound-free.

There's a sign.

SORRY, THE PANDAS ARE OUT TODAY!

There are pictures.

"Ming Ming and Shing Hua." They are curled up next to one another—all black and white and velvety. As if a giant patchwork quilt were draped over them. They blend. They're in love. They look like paid panda bear models from the bridal magazines.

I sit and watch the empty exhibit all day. I watch the waterfalls run and the bamboo sway and the manmade stream look so natural leaking along through the enclosure. I watch, and every once in a while, every few breezes that blow, a leaf will move or a twig will crack, and I, with my sunglasses on and my commemorative panda bear cup locked in-between my thighs, will look up hoping to see them frolicking in their cage. Running over rocks and ducking into caves, giddy with love, oblivious to the crowd that has drawn outside of their pretty, pretty cage. And how they'll play, how they'll look so content exchanging branches like they were popsicles, a gesture of love only a panda bear can make. And the Chinese government will be so proud, and the zoo keepers will sigh so deep, and all the teachers and mothers and buses, buses full of kids, will be crying—weeping really—to have found the two pandas playing together inside their cage.

At two o'clock a zookeeper comes to hose down their empty cage. "They won't be out today." He looks young.

"I know," I say.

At three o'clock, I follow a field trip of four-year-olds over to the elephant's cage. The elephants do tricks, the people clap. Everyone laughs.

"Tell me what the pandas did today." Steve is soft with the washcloth on my face.

I lift my chin, the warm water stings. "The pandas were out today." The way Steve pauses to listen to me, the way his hand on my face doesn't make me afraid, and the way the water sounds running in the sink makes sense, complete and perfect sense. And I pretend for a moment that the pandas were just out on a panda bear sort of date and that he wasn't still beating the shit out of her behind the closed doors of their pretty, pretty cage.

Steve wipes the rest of the blood off my face. "Now, there," he says, and kisses me.

"Did you know an elephant can stand on one leg?"

APPLICATION PROCESS

My father left when I was ten. Bet our whole savings in a poker game at the Flamingo. I told Victor when I applied for the job that my interest in casinos goes way back. Of course, after what my father thought was an almost unbeatable four of a kind (jack high), my mother never talked to him again. Christmas cards, birthday cards—I heard from him twice a year. Three times the year I was eighteen and out in Arizona, out of money and out on the street, minus the boyfriend who promised to marry me if I moved in with him. "Dad." Called him collect. "Can you help me?"

"Princess." He sounded old. "If I help you, can you stop by with some gin?"

I forgave my father. For the Flamingo, my birthdays, the gin. *Face it, Ginger: sometimes the ante is already in.*

When Susan and Al got married, everyone said it wouldn't last. Even with the unity candle and the white doves and the 'oh, how everyone cried.' There was just something that told you that later he'd be fucking a Zodiac showgirl in room 15 of the Comfort Inn, just off the 10.

I don't imagine, if Steve ever asks me to marry him, that we'll have the perfect marriage. We won't look like the Ralph Lauren sheet ad in this month's issue of *Martha Stewart Wedding*: the couple in the Hamptons, lying in the sand. We'll look more like the pandas on the ten o'clock news, trying to find new ways to avoid each other in an already small space.

I don't imagine us vacationing in the Bahamas, or even in Lake Tahoe for that matter. We'll probably forget to start a retirement plan. I don't suspect that Steve will suddenly come home every night at ten, sober, or that he'll stop hitting me or that I'll stop cocktailing, or that Susan will stop cooking or that Mom will stop buying her nasal inhalers in three's. Our wedding, even if we do release two white doves, won't make Dad call more than once a year. But I imagine it will change things a bit. Just a little, maybe. Like when the pandas finally fuck—won't everyone who's been watching experience some type of climax with them?

"He doesn't have a kind face," my mother says. "You should never marry him."

Rather than inappropriately reminding her how much we all loved Al's face; how, when I was young, everyone said, 'you can tell from your father's face that he's a good man'; I tell her, "Well, Mom, that's just too damn bad. He's the only face I have."

FOOD HANDLERS' CARD:
All employees must take and pass the Tribal Food Handling test with a score of ninety percent or better.
   Question One:
   Once opened, perishable food will last for how long?
   a) twenty-four hours b) one week to ten days c) no more than a few days

   He's keeping the food from her. On his side of the cage. This is on Sunday's front page.
   Because of an inefficient intestinal system the panda must feed for 12 to 16 hours a day.

THE LOS ANGELES TIMES *GOES ON TO SAY:*
Without the ability to consume 22 to 40 pounds of bamboo each day, Ming Ming will not only be unable to mate, but will eventually starve to death. The fate of this panda as well as their entire species seems to be at stake.

   They're getting good at this game of chess. He moves clockwise, she moves counter-clockwise. He jumps up on a rock, she jumps away. They sleep apart, she sleeps with one eye open. This is not a joke. Here's the quote from the front page: "Ming Ming Sleeps With One Eye Open."
   They photographed her. She looks painfully alive and un-rehearsed.
   "Look, Mom." I try to show her the picture.
   "I can't look." After dinner, my mom cries and says it hurts to see me this way. "I can't take much more of this, Ginger."
   "Me neither," I say. Though I don't think she's referring to Ming Ming's inability to sleep with both eyes closed. I'm assuming it has something to do with the ten pounds of make-up I've piled on my face.
   "Why do you let him treat you this way?" Susan cuts the homemade apple pie.
   It's filled with three kinds of apples: Granny Smith, Red Delicious and Gala. She's made both homemade whipped cream and homemade vanilla ice cream. She's grated the cinnamon from cinnamon sticks. "Good question, Susan." I take a piece. "Why *do you* let him treat you this way?"

My mom dries her eyes and takes a piece of Susan's pie. She takes a cleansing breath. Therapy habits are hard to break. "What else does the article have to say?"

We all read.

We all eat.

We all say, "What great pie."

"They need to put some food on her side of the cage." I pick up the knife and slice another piece. I watch the crust crumble and break.

Susan picks up the paper. "Yeah, I mean how long can she really sleep like that?"

c) *no more than a few days*

SICK DAYS AND PERSONAL TIME
After a three-month probationary period each employee will receive three sick days per year. Sick days must be requested at least twenty-four hours in advance and approved by an immediate supervisor. No personal time will be given to any employee; personal issues should be handled on sick days.

The second time I go to see the pandas, I call in sick.

"You can't call in sick."

"I know."

"You never call in sick."

"I know."

"Waitresses don't call in sick." Victor is talking with his mouth full.

"I'm sick."

"Well, get over it."

"I will."

I pretend he knows I'm going to see the bears. "Buy me a postcard." I will. "Take lots of pictures." I will. "Tell her to get over it and move to the other side of the fucking cage." I will.

It's easier to pretend like this than to feel bad for what Victor really says.

"Feel better."

"I will."

Victor doesn't say this either, but I've spent enough days feeling bad for the shit that people really say.

While in front of the cage, I wish I brought a measuring tape. It's hard to measure the length of something so large by merely estimation. I walk the length ten times until twice I come up with eighteen feet, heel to toe, heel to toe. I decide it's half the size of my trailer, not including the covered patio.

Shing Hua, the male, follows me as I walk, heel to toe, heel to toe. He's pacing, watching me. I pretend not to see him, but with each step I take, I can hear his paw pad hit the cement flooring at the very edge of the cage. His fur is pressed up against the glass and it looks flat and smashed. *"Giant Pandas have short claws and plantigrade feet."* These are *"Panda Facts"* posted all over the cage. *"Both heel and toe make contact with the ground when walking, a manner similar to humans."* It makes a thud, his paw, on the edge of their extravagant cage.

Ming Ming is behind a row of bare bamboo at the back of their cage. She's beautiful and still, like an elaborate china vase; her eyes, like tiny black pebbles, are vacant and haunted. She's eaten all of the bamboo leaves and has been gnawing on sticks for days. Other than the occasional glimpse of her perfectly patterned face, or the trampled grass on which she lies, one would hardly know she's there. One would never expect to find two bears in this cage.

By one-thirty, the male has paced the length of the cage two hundred and forty-one times. He has eaten twenty-eight stalks of bamboo.

"She'll never come out," I say.

The young keeper comes in at eleven, two, and four to hose down the cage.

"She's afraid." This time he looks at me when I speak.

"Are you talking about Ming Ming?"

"Yes." He uses a very powerful hose to wash down the cage.

"They're doing fine now." He looks away.

"She doesn't look fine."

"She refuses to eat." Can he be any more than sixteen? "She's just hungry, that's all."

"Then why don't you put some food on her side of the cage?"

"There are no sides." Water is pouring out everywhere. The male's pads are now making a squishing sound as he paces.

"You know that's not true." I'm sitting on the bench with a stack of brochures. I've been studying them all day. I've come twice now—I've called in sick, I've driven on the 5, and all the zoo can do is send out a sixteen-year old boy three times a day.

"We don't want to interfere."

"With what?"

"Their mating."

"I think we both know they're not going to mate."

"What do you know, lady?" And he starts to walk away.

"Don't walk away from me." I get up, my brochures and papers scatter all over the cement; a few fly into the cage. "I know this isn't about two panda bears fucking." I am walking towards him. "I know this isn't about her"—I point—"starving while you stand here and wash their shit away." A mother hushes her children and hurries them by the cage. "Why don't you just move it for her? Put a few trees over there? Just give her a fighting chance." Shing Hua has stopped pacing altogether now and is staring at me, listening to me yell.

"I'm calling security," the hose boy says.

"Just give her one fucking break," I say. "Just one fucking chance." And then, as if I have no control over it, I start to cry.

"I'm calling security," he says again.

"I heard you," I shout.

Shing Hua resumes his pacing and I'm still crying as people laugh and clap in front of the elephant's cage.

When the head zoo keeper arrives with security and they escort me from the cage, I watch the water continue to pour and Shing Hua continue to pace and the bamboo leaves blow in excess on his side of the cage.

"So, what's your name?" I ask the hose boy.

"Jeremiah."

And everything seems to go still, to stop, for just a few seconds—maybe no more than two. And in those two seconds, from far across the cage, Ming Ming bolts from behind the bamboo and makes a run for the stacks and stacks of food.

"Do you like working with the panda bears, Jeremiah?"

We watch her eat.

"They're not bears. Not technically. More like raccoons."

Shing Hua waits patiently until she's in close range.

"Oh," I say.

"Don't worry, most people make that mistake."

Waits, until she's just inches away.

DRUG TESTING: POLICY AND PROCEDURE

A mandatory drug test will be administered to all employees once a month at random. A positive test result will lead to immediate termination.

When I was sixteen, my best friend, Jason Contor, and James Lincoln, my boyfriend, snuck into the belly of the dinosaur off the 10. The Brontosaurus is a gift shop from the base of his esophagus to the tip of his colon. There are stairs that take you through what would be his main intestine.

"Here." Jason passed the joint.

His father managed the gift shop. Once or twice a month, we would go there at night and get lit.

"Good shit," James said, pounding the side of the Dinosaur. "Sorry sons of bitches."

I took a hit.

"You know they'd still be around if they'd just fucked each other more."

"Profound," I told James. "Really profound." I hated Marijuana Enlightenment almost as much as the munchies. I was 15 pounds overweight by my senior year.

"Can you imagine being the last two dinosaurs on earth?" Jason had the joint again. "The pressure alone probably killed them."

"No shit," James said. The dinosaur's belly was full of smoke. "Hey, Ginger. Wanna save the human race?"

"What's the point, James?" I got up to leave. "Once something needs to be saved, it's already too late."

"See," Jason said, "that kind of negative thinking is exactly what fried these guys."

I drive by those dinosaurs every goddamn day, twice a day, on the way to the casino. Jason and James never did graduate.

JOB ADVANCEMENT
The Zodiac Casino will compensate any employee, partially, for the furthering of their education in order to advance their careers.

In my English class at the junior college, the professor asks us to write what we know. "Write what you know," he says.

"This doesn't fulfill the assignment," he remarks when I turn in a paper about the pandas. "What do you know about panda bears?"

"They're not bears." I take my paper back.

"Why don't you write about your career, Ginger." He loosens his tie and leans on the desk. "You're a dancer over at the Zodiac right?" He picks at his fingernails with a pocketknife.

"Cocktail waitress."

"Whatever. Write about your career." He smiles. "I bet you have some great material there." He puts the blade under the nail and digs.

And I think for a moment before answering him. I think about my career and my relationship with Steve and all the different foods Susan has made in the last few weeks. I look at the knife and say, "All right." And then I breathe. "We have old ladies that piss on themselves at the slots, men with their hand up my ass, kids left in cars when it's one hundred and five outside. How's that for material, Professor Green?" He looks surprised. "We have pink slips on the blackjack tables, social security checks cashed by Ada, the change girl with the red hair. She's quite a character." I take another breath and Professor Green looks at me, then makes a reassuring gesture to the class. "Maybe I should write about the number of times I've tried to quit, walked right into Victor's office—he's the pit boss—only to stop and see myself in that little mirror, the one I'm convinced he puts there on purpose, to see myself and realize, with my black roots and blonde hair, that this just may be as good as it gets. Number of times I've done that? Twenty-two times."

"Ginger." He's holding his hands in front of him. He's dropped the pocketknife.

"I should write about the conversations I have with Steve when he's drunk. Steve's my boyfriend—he eats macaroni and cheese. When I pretend I'm asleep, he's wonderful. Real sweet. He says we should elope, we should go to Vegas. Too bad the Zodiac doesn't have one of those all night wedding chapels, huh? Elvis could do the vows. Wouldn't everyone always remember our wedding if Elvis did the vows? But this isn't Vegas, this is Morongo. And Elvis'll never marry me in a designer wedding gown in the 2.5 million-dollar lobby of the Bellagio. Did I ever tell you about the showgirl who cut up her husband's hand?"

Professor Green just shakes his head.

I stare at him a few moments before turning around to grab my bag.

"I forgive you." The entire room is quiet.

"For what?" he asks.

"For calling what I do a career."

EMERGENCY EXITS

The Zodiac Casino is equipped with four emergency exits in addition to the ten exits located at the north, north-west, west, south-west, south-east sides of the casino. In the event of an emergency such as fire, earthquake or power failure please proceed calmly to the nearest exit.

In the kitchen we're sweating and I'm chopping roma tomatoes for the spaghetti.

"I can't believe this fucking thing is out again." Steve is leaning against the wall, his face pressed close to the vent of the swamp cooler that's spitting out hot, moist air. I see him out of the corner of my eye but am more interested in the tomato on the cutting board than in his bitching.

"It doesn't work when it's humid out." I have way too many tomatoes here. "I told you that."

Swamp coolers, like trailers, are popular in the desert—they're more efficient and less expensive than air-conditioning units. The concept is simple: outside air is sucked through a wet sponge, cooled, and then circulated into the inside air. It only works with hot, dry air.

"I tell you that every year."

"Well, that must mean it's always this fucking hot in here every year." Steve hits the side of the cooler and I jump. "What a piece of shit." There's really only so much transformation that can be done. Even with air.

"Turn up the TV, please," I ask him from the kitchen. The pandas are on and they have now entitled it: "Panda Crisis 2003." A colorful graphic flashes above the newscaster's head.

"Turn it up yourself." Steve hits the cooler again. This time I don't flinch.

"Stop it," I say.

"Fuck you," he says.

My hands are covered in tomato flesh and skin.

Steve is so close to the vent, panting so hard, that his breath is spilling all over the cooler. The room is filling with the stench of his gut, the two six packs of beer.

"Turn it off," he yells. "You're obsessed with that shit."

"No," I say. I'm chopping the tomatoes as fast as I can.

"*What* did you say?" He lets go of the vent and walks toward me.

They don't show Ming Ming on TV anymore. She's too damaged, too thin. Mosquitoes are eating away the tops of her ears and making nests in her raw skin. This is what www.pandacam.com said.

Steve's in the kitchen now, right up next to me. "I said, turn it off!" he yells in my ear.

Shing Hua, however, is fat and pacing. He is posing for pictures and being adored by little kids. The newscaster smiles, and though I can't read his lips, I'm sure he's saying something dreadfully clever like, "Shing Hua is just afraid to commit." The whole news desk laughs.

Steve grabs a beer and looks at my tits. "By the way, how are they?"

"Fine," I say, and look down at the knife and the whole red mess.

"You know I love you?" And he kisses me on the neck.

"I know."

I'm already sorry there are no tomatoes left.

TERMINATION
Casino employees will be escorted immediately from the premises by security should there be grounds for termination.

THE GIANT PANDAS

In line at the Zodiac, Linda asks, "Did you hear?"

"I heard."

"They're sending Ming Ming back."

"Yeah," I say. "She was starving to death on the other side of the cage." I hand my bag to Bill. "I heard it last night on the news."

"Fuck that," Linda says. "I would have done anything to get that food from him. She was just going to lay down and die."

Bill reaches deep into my bag. Why does he look so surprised?

"Face it Linda," I say, "sometimes the ante is already in."

It was hard for them to prove whose fingers those really were. Steve ran off late that night, scared that, before stitching up his hand, they'd ask him about the bruise on my cheek and my cracked ribs (which they now tell me will take two months to heal). Besides, *They have their own law there. Their own police. They have their own police cars.* Mom was right. My boobs are healed enough to strip and Susan has entered her Pumpkin Crème Brulee in a local contest. I bet she wins.

No charges pressed, just some mandatory counseling sessions and a promise to never step foot inside the casino again.

I tell the therapist what he needs to hear. Yes, I couldn't take it anymore. No, I don't remember it. No, I don't feel like I'm capable of doing something like that ever again.

"What was it with those panda bears?" he asks.

"They're not bears," I say.

"What ever happened to her?"

"The day they were to ship her back, the keepers found them sleeping together in the corner of their cage."

"Imagine that." He adjusts his glasses. "Just when everyone gave up on them."

"After lunch she killed him."

"Are you making this up?"

"Imagine that." I adjust my short skirt. "Just when everyone thought she'd be rescued in the end."

HABIT TRAIL

We've managed to lose the hamster, Fluffy, again. Of course it'll be my job to find him. Of course this occurs at 7 a.m.

The alarm goes off at five, and I'm immediately resentful of the gym shoes laid out by the bed the night before. The gym shoes are a reminder that after our trip to Disneyland last weekend, the fat somehow gathered over the edge of my Victoria's Secret Boxer Shorts For Her. I get up, step over the gym shoes, and go back to bed. The alarm goes off again at six. I'm already late and running the shower for my husband, Simon, who has, like me, no intention of getting out of bed. I throw the gym shoes at him.

"Get up." I hop by Simon wearing one fluffy pink bunny slipper that our three-year-old got me for Mother's Day. "It's Monday. I have PTA." She always giggles to see me in them. "I have to be there by eight." Right now I only wear one, but she'll giggle still.

This is what three-year-olds do—giggle and ask questions you'll never have the answers to. Why do zebras have stripes? Why is the sky blue? I've heard them all. I make up the answers, too.

"I'm up," Simon says, and, like most mornings, he manages to roll over, get up, and walk naked to the shower. I manage not to notice him. His nakedness. He manages not to care. We manage to continue like this, not noticing each other throughout toothpaste, hair gel, hair spray, deodorant, *where's my comb, in the bottom drawer,* mouthwash, dental floss and *I love you Rebecca, I love you too, drive safe.* We're experts at management like this.

In the den, my six-year-old is in her pajamas eating peanut butter out of the jar with both hands. "Sissy's still sleeping," she says. I scoop her up and head to the kitchen, over the laundry basket that hasn't held clean laundry in what I imagine to be over a year, over the newspapers piled on the floor; and, with one foot still tucked away in a bunny slipper (though I am now in an oxford shirt and khaki skirt), and one hand free, I manage to pry open the refrigerator door; I replace the peanut butter, take out the milk, and rinse off the six-year old in the sink.

"Mommy," the six-year-old says, "Fluffy got out again."

Of course this has to happen at 7 a.m. on a PTA morning.

"Try the hamper," I say, since this is where most of our domesticated rodents seem to escape: Templeton the rat, Whiskey the mouse, Tweedle-Dee and Tweedle-Dum the matching guinea pigs (though they made it all the way from the hamper to the dryer in one fell swoop and never re-gained consciousness). "I'll help you look later." All that spinning. "Get ready for school." Can never be good for the brain, even if it's a very tiny rodent brain.

At the preschool, I drop off the three-year-old. "Sissy," all the charming preschool teachers say. I smile though I know that, as soon as I leave, they'll drop my child—the one they're so preciously cooing over while I stand here—and they'll find a good corner, get a good chair, read a good book, and, from where they sit, will watch Sissy for five hours until I pick her up; then they'll begin to coo all over her again.

"Good-bye, baby," I say. She waves.

Wave. Giggle, ask unanswerable questions, and wave. I realize this is a pretty important formula for girls, a Miss America prerequisite I'm afraid.

At Monte Vista Elementary School, I'm able to drop Ryann off in the round drive, as she is six. "Be careful as you cross."

"I will."

As if their critical judgment skills have not yet kicked in at five and a half, five and three quarters, five and one-eighth. Perhaps at six, if their brains are knocked out by an on-coming SUV, the school will not assume any legal responsibility, as the *look-both-ways-before-you-cross* and the *speed-at-which-an-object-approaches* lessons have been put into those brains—and both prior to the Mayflower parade and macaroni Christmas Construct.

"Look for Fluffy."

"I will." I won't.

I won't because I'm not going home. I'm not turning left at the stop sign. In fact, I turn right. Turn right toward the intersection at Warner and Main. I won't stop at the Vons on the left to pick up chicken for tonight's dinner, I won't make a broccoli and cheese casserole; I will of course forget the salad and burn the rolls just like I do every Monday night. PTA night. I keep heading past the bakery with those delicious little tiramisu cakes that Simon loves, past the post office and the Taco Bell. I pull into the driveway on my right, and stop next to the blue Ford Explorer in the parking lot of the Motel 6.

Of course there's no PTA.

Mondays at 8 a.m. I wait in the parking lot of the Motel 6, next to the blue Ford Explorer. I think it's maybe the hotel manager's car, or perhaps the owner's. Actually, I don't know if anyone really owns these motels, takes pride in the possession of rooms rented by the hour, but it's a nice car nonetheless—a car that claims importance. Always clean, tinted windows. I pretend like I've never looked inside, but I have. I've seen the CD player and the car seat and the empty Burger King bag. For eight months, I've imagined what the owner of the Explorer must be like.

I imagine every Monday while waiting the usual ten minutes. In eight months of Mondays—in three hundred and twenty minutes—I have decided that the owner is a she, and she eats a Sausage Croissant with a diet soda each morning before parking her car here. I imagine her (because it's funny) owning a pet monkey that sits in the car seat and accompanies her across the street to work at the dog groomers. The monkey helps her brush the dogs—he especially likes to tie pretty pink bows in even the boy dogs' hair.

I look in my rear-view mirror for the drapes in room 26A to open.

I could've imagined more in these three hundred and twenty minutes but a pretty pink bow is as far as I get before realizing that, when I leave my car—when Daniel pulls the cords on the drapes from room 26A—someone out there will be imagining what the owner of this Camry is doing between the hours of nine and noon. Do they imagine Daniel's fingers through my hair, my legs wrapped tightly around his neck? To leave a *Blues Clues* book on the dash, a box of Goldfish crackers on the seat, and an empty pack of cigarettes spilling tobacco crumbs onto the baby seat in the back—what must she do?

I will remember to dispose of the cigarette box before I pick up the three-year old, before I make the chicken and broccoli casserole, before I hang the finger-painting on the fridge, before I tell my husband I can't find the hamster again.

The Motel 6 is much less sleazy than you would imagine. There are no quarter machines bedside, there are no stains on the carpet, no condoms in the bathroom. There's actually something very soothing about the simplicity, the implication of domesticity, within the Motel 6 decor. The quilted bedspread that's only an eighth of an inch thick, the paisley shade of the glued-down lamp, the pretty pen and paper set on the night stand. (As if it would be the most normal thing in the world, to sit down and write a letter to someone, a postcard of my affair, saying, "Wish You Were Here.")

Daniel's telling me about a girl in the pastrami shop who thought he looked like Don Johnson—"You know, from *Miami Vice*"—while we're fucking atop the king-sized bed's quilted comforter.

"Yeah, he's on *Nash Bridges*," I say.

Of course, we're at the end of our affair.

"It happens," I will say, inside this same motel room, many days from now.

"We knew it couldn't last," he'll say. "Not like it was," he'll say. He'll be naked on the bed because we'll fuck several times more before either one of us says good-bye on that day, many days from now.

"Never like it was," I'll say, and we'll both be thinking about those first few Mondays when, sitting in my Camry and staring at the rearview, it took all of me to keep from gasping the minute I saw the curtains part. And we'll both be thinking about the shower door that broke when we pressed against it too hard, too many times, too many Mondays ago when it rained all day, rained so hard you could barely see. And we'll remember how we laughed the next Monday when the door had been replaced with a plastic shower curtain covered in large bright tropical fish. How we laughed when you said, "Well, I guess that just about covers that."

"But it was fun."

"A blast." That's what I'll say before I start to cry. Before I start to pretend that I didn't know this. That I didn't know that once the excitement of fucking someone new fades away, you'll inevitably begin to make small talk during sex, make plans for next week, find something to watch on TV for the last two hours (I mean you have the room from nine to noon anyway). I'll pretend I didn't know that, at the end of every affair, the unspoken guarantee is that you'll both be left with nothing more than the choice to stay or leave.

And talking about Don Johnson's career while your lover comes isn't enough to leave the life you have for the life you've made in room 26A.

"I love you," Daniel says.

"I love you too."

Not even this will make you stay.

Though today will not be the day I make that choice. Today I ignore the occasional sounds of cars passing on the highway and appreciate instead the hum of the tiny bathroom's fluorescent light. Today we lay naked atop the bed and I find the bedspread's thick wax-like threads comfortable, and not irritating. Today I don't talk about peanut butter hands or the lost bunny slipper or the matinee of *A Bug's Life 2* that I'll catch this Saturday.

"Still calling it PTA?"

"Yeah." I laugh and appreciate how light Daniel's hand feels on my leg. How soft, like butterfly wings or cotton balls.

"What does that stand for anyway?"

"Parent Teachers Association." I put my hand on top his and notice how small mine is in comparison. "But I don't think it means that anymore, really." I'm reminded of my husband and my three-year-old and that game they play: *paper covers rock*. Her hand barely able to cover his knuckles.

"Kinda like the YMCA."

Mr. Yamashiro from the dry-cleaner's calls me "Mrs. *Mow*-llen," which sounds very different from the pharmacist's "Mrs. Mullen." I like going to see Mr. Yamashiro on the way home from 26A because he calls me this. He always lets me borrow his pen, no matter that I have two in my purse, no matter that I have hand-washed that silk blouse in the past. "You look very beautiful today Mrs. *Mow*-llen." I always ask to borrow his pen to write my check, no matter that I have cash.

"So you're having an affair with Mr. Yamashiro, the dry-cleaning guy?" Angela meets me at Starbucks on Tuesdays and Thursdays when there's no PTA.

"No." I hate cappuccinos, lattes, café mochas, Frappuccinos—just more names. "Black coffee," I say, and the master-brewer hardly knows what to do. "Black coffee? Would you like our Breakfast Blend, Seasonal Blend, or Premium French Roast today?"

"Okay," I say.

"Should you really have this much affection for your dry-cleaner, Rebecca?" She pulls a twenty out of her purse. "Non-fat Grande Café Mocha." She's so good at this. Of course Angela has no kids. "Extra chocolate." Of course Angela is rail-thin.

"He's just a nice man."

"You wouldn't want to fuck him." She holds up her pinky finger and the master-brewer laughs while handing her her change.

"Nice, Angela." I take my black coffee over to an oversized couch with an overstuffed pillow.

"Maybe you shouldn't see him anymore." We sit down.

"Oh for God's sake, Angela, stop." The coffee is hot. "I'm not having an affair with the dry-cleaning man."

"I mean maybe you shouldn't see *him* anymore."

Quickly, in fractions of a second, I play out every time I've pulled in to the Motel 6, every time I've exited, every time we were careless by the door when saying goodbye, every time I knocked before the curtains were pulled. "Who?" I say.

"Whoever it is that's making you so sad."

The coffee is suddenly thick and shitty and my stomach turns.

"I'm not sad."

"It's always sad to want what you'll never let yourself have."

And I suppose it's in this moment that I should be thankful for how well Angela knows me, how long we've been friends, how clearly she sees how sad I am.

"Did I tell you Ryann's hamster got out again?"

"Did you check the dryer?" She has foam on her lips and it looks lovely. "Remember those poor fucking guinea pigs?" She laughs.

"It wasn't as funny as I made it out to be."

Ryann believes the hamster has found another home, maybe even one right down the street, with a bigger habit-trail and lots of friends.

"Do you think they put Fluffy in the ball at his new house?" This is what Ryann believes because this is what I said.

"I think he has a bigger ball there." This is what I said because Fluffy is what I found trapped in-between the entertainment center and the living room wall when I was looking for Sissy's *Barney* tape.

"Now, sleep tight." His eyes were wide open. He was clinging to the wall for his dear, dear life.

"Don't let the bed bugs bite." She giggles. "I love you, Mom."

Rigor mortis had already set in and the damn thing wouldn't budge. I imagine there was a moment when he was regretful for having left his habit-trail, a moment when he realized his little rodent claws wouldn't cling to the wall forever and that soon he would slide down, way down, until his body got lodged between the wood and the wall. I imagine he missed his water bottle and salt lick, the comforts a hamster might have from being caged in.

I had to wait until Simon was home, until the kids were in bed. When we were tiptoeing and peering over the top of the edge of the entertainment center, a feather duster in Simon's hand and a plastic grocery bag on the floor. We laughed just like one would to see a dead hamster suspended in what seemed to be mid-air.

"It's just that he looks so terrified."

"I know." It really was a laugh-cry.

"How long do you think he hung on there?" He says this in a whisper, and I notice for the first time the way his lip drops after he pronounces the 'r' at the end of a word. *There.* Just a slight drop. *There, here, where.*

"Oh, God, this is awful." I close my eyes and turn my head.

When the hamster drops into the plastic bag, I jump and hit my knee on the corner of the entertainment center. Simon drops the feather duster. It lands on the hamster and we both gasp, then laugh, then say, "Shhhh, you'll wake the kids." I'm not sorry for the lie I told Ryann about the habit-trail dream house and the little hamster friends. I think I might've even said that they feed him nuts there. I'm not sorry for that, because kids don't know how to laugh-cry, not until the age of ten at least.

Tonight, beneath the blankets and the sheets and the duvet cover that matches the curtains we bought at Cost Plus last Christmas, the details of how it all happened don't seem as important. The mutual friend, the coincidences and chance meetings, the "we really have to stop bumping into each other like this." Is that really the start of an affair? Or is it when you start to shop at the market twelve miles away because you know he'll be there buying the cured ham and the Haagen Daz and the orange juice you told him was better. "It's fortified," you said. Fortified juice certainly can't be the start of an affair. No, maybe it's when he begins to call your house—your house with your kids—and you have a code name. *Is Jose there?* How deep your heart hurts and for so many things when you hear Simon say, *no Jose lives here.* Perhaps it's even before this, before the curtains are pulled and the exceptions are made, perhaps it's when the washer breaks and the baby throws up and *the gas man will come between nine and five, so you should be home all day*—perhaps it's even before this. Before weeks go by and neither you nor Simon has noticed that you're making love on a schedule like trash days. Once a week, sometimes less. Sometimes you just forget to take out the trash. Yes, maybe this is the start of an affair—when someone simply forgets to take out the trash.

In the morning, I'll tell Simon about the dream I had about the hamster.
"Fluffy?" he'll ask.
"I was in his cage," I'll say.
"It must've been a pretty big cage." He'll be shaving I suppose.
"And he asked me if I was unhappy in there."
He'll nick the underpart of his chin.
"I told him not so unhappy."
And, I'll hold a piece of toilet paper to his bleeding chin.

ADVICE FOR THE BRIDE

ON HER WEDDING DAY

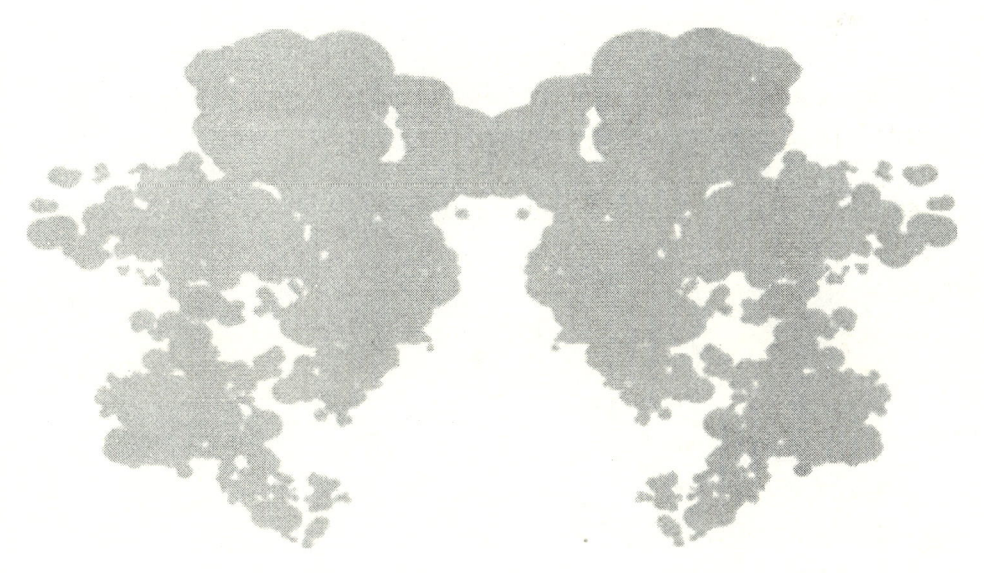

They tell you about the vows, the shoes, the flowers, and the cake. They'll offer opinions, whether to hire a DJ or a string quartet. You'll hear the story about birds' bellies bursting and you'll throw birdseed rather than rice on your wedding day. Make sure your dress fits snugly, but not *too* snugly. "Can you dance in it?" Someone will surely ask you this.

"Are you leaving?"
"I think I've just about got everything for the night."
"O.K."
"Good-bye." Sal leaves through the front door. "You'll kiss Kate and tell her…"
"Good-bye," I say. We're pretending. We're pretending it's just any other day—not the morning we eat bagels together, file for divorce, and then go our separate ways. Still, Sal will be back tonight and almost every night. To make things easier on Kate, he will eat dinner with us during the week; read to her; say, "Good Night Moon, Good Night Stars"; kiss her; and tuck her in. To make things easier on Kate, I will cook dinner—salmon and fresh asparagus, I suppose. I might even make a dessert: fruit torte or pecan pie. To make things easier on Kate, Sal will eat everything on his plate, leave at nine, and be fast asleep on his girlfriend's tits by ten. Yes, this will be best for Kate.

Of course, they'll mention your hair. Something simple yet sophisticated. An up-do, maybe. "Think Audrey Hepburn," said my sister-in-law Sophie, though her hair wasn't sophisticated or swept up in any way when she got married. From the looks of the pictures, she'd just stepped out of the pool. ("That's the wonderful thing about Vegas," Sophie said.) One day, I'll be sure to tell my daughter, after she knows her ABC's and doesn't sing Barney songs anymore, that it's O.K. to be in a bikini on your wedding day.

"How are you doing?" What everyone asks.
"Fine." What everyone wants me to say.
Though I'm not doing so well, I think. I start a load of laundry and make Kate a pink cake with silver sprinkles for her pre-school carnival. (Erin Dennis' mom is bringing in their cat dressed up as a lion.) I ask Sal if

he'll attend. He tells me he doesn't think so. He's trying to move on. "It's probably better if we don't act like a couple anymore." I say fine. I say I understand. But I'm not moving on. I'm not having dinner with friends. I'm still going to bed at night, waiting to hear the lock turn, waiting to watch his shadow creep in. I'm still making too many eggs in the morning, I'm still setting the washing machine on Large Load. I let Kate lick the icing from the bowl with her hands.

"Let him put some on your face," my maid of honor, Heddy, advised while picking out the cake topper at Party World on the corner of Central and Brand. "All his friends will be egging him on." She fondled the neck of two glass swans with her fingers. "If he doesn't, he'll feel weak. If he does"—she handed me the swans—"keep smiling. Everyone will be waiting for you to act like a bitch and wipe it off."
"Do you know swans are the only birds that are monogamous?"
"Gerbils are too."
"Gerbils aren't birds," I said.
"What does it matter?" She whipped out her credit card. "We aren't either."

For Kate's first birthday, Sal bought her a rabbit.
"I don't think this is practical for a one-year-old." It was amazing how he always made me look this way: uptight, restrictive. Tension a one-year-old can't begin to comprehend yet can feel when her parents give her separate birthday gifts. "Who'll clean up after it?" I tied three balloons on the banister of the staircase.
"They're not messy like other rodents." Sal loved pleasing Kate this way. "They can learn to go in a litter box."
"Who'll teach it?"
"Oh Christ, Helen." He picked up Kate, the clinging bunny too. "You never used to be this way."

I hear the laundry cycle spin.

I think it was my Auntie Pat who made sure I had something old, something borrowed, something blue. My grandfather put a World War Two penny in my left shoe, cried, and, before I could even thank him, left the room. My mother came in and I asked her to put out the cigarette.

"Don't forget to wrap a tissue around your bouquet."

"Have you been drinking?" I asked.

"Just a few." Her dress was fuchsia.

When my grandfather died last summer in the middle of that horrible heat wave, Sal didn't even come to the funeral. He said it was too depressing. Funny thing about funerals—if you're not looking at the coffin or standing by the buffet, it's very reminiscent of a wedding day.

Sara came over at two. I woke up from a long dry nap and Sara said, "Looks like you haven't slept in days." She was wearing a two-piece suit with no pantyhose. "Where's Kate?"

"Sleeping," I said. "Since when do you wear a suit with bare legs?"

"I'm taking her for a couple hours." Sara looked so awkward with a child. "Pull yourself together. Break something. Scream. Burn a few of his things." She readjusted Kate on her bare, bare legs. "She doesn't need to see you this way."

I've known Sara almost all my life. We were neighbors at the house on Pine Cone; she gave me my first Barbie. I gave it back to her as a keepsake when her parents split up and she moved to Pasadena. I laughed until I cried when she brought Barbie to the Rehearsal Dinner in a full-length candlelight-wedding gown.

"Waterproof mascara."

"I don't think I'll cry."

"You will." She gave me two tubes, and mumbled as she dug for the third: "I was like a fountain on my wedding day."

Sara was like a fountain on all three of her wedding days.

In the shower, I wasn't worried about Kate, though I hadn't even washed my hair in three days. Kids care so little about life's major catastrophes. Kate just wants to eat her morning bowl of Cheerios with a fork and butter knife instead of a spoon. She couldn't care less that her daddy fucked a candy-striper in the hospital elevator last spring.

I saw my father last. He joked at first when he came into the room. "We can still get out of here, Princess."

"Daddy." I could see he wanted to cry.

"He'll hate it when you tell him to take out the trash."

I laughed. "Then *I'll* take out the trash."

My father smiled and someone snapped a picture, though I was sure we were alone. "It'll make you bitter," my father said. And, in that ridiculously adorable bridal suite, he breathed deeply, then exhaled all that he'd been holding in throughout his eighteen years of marriage to my mother.

"Are you ready to give me away?" As he leaned over to kiss me, I smiled and pretended, pretended, he had said better—not bitter. "It'll make you better."

Too many times to count, I've looked for the picture that captured the look on my face when I asked my dad to give me away. I'd kill to know if I looked anything like I did when Sal said, "You and Kate should keep the house. I'll find someplace else to stay."

When Sal finally leaves—really leaves—he should take all the CD's we bought together, the stereo too. All his friends will be egging him on and I wouldn't want anyone to think that I was a bitch.

I forget to fold the laundry.

I sit down and eat Kate's silver and pink carnival cake.

SHOPPING

THE MALL

Call it a coincidence. Call it irony, call it dumb luck. Remember when you're calling it this that your sister always said: if it weren't for dumb luck, you'd have no luck at all. Tell yourself it has nothing to do with you—it's not your fault. Don't do anything drastic, don't change your hair, don't go on a crash diet, don't buy a new car. You're still growing out your hair and making car payments from the last time you told yourself it wasn't your fault.

The mall doesn't open until ten am.

So what you're doing now is standing outside the mall. With a small group of people, medicated like farm animals, waiting to go in. You're ordering coffee and pastries from an outdoor bakery stand with your niece, Nan. Nan says she knows the boy selling the coffee and pastries. She orders a Diet Coke and says, "Hi Stan," then leans into you and whispers, "Everyone calls him 'The Edge.'"

You order a cafe latte and an apricot scone. "How do you know him?"

"We're in detention together."

"Oh."

He has black hair, one piercing above his eyebrow, and he's thin. Too thin and too tall for his frame—as if right there, behind the green-canopied wood cart, he's growing out of his skin.

He hands you a black coffee and a plain donut.

You thank The Edge. You say, "What a coincidence."

"What is?"

"That you know him."

"Oh," Nan says.

Outside the mall at five to ten, standing on painted concrete in front of a store with amber glass, staring at two naked mannequins with purses around their necks, you call it all coincidence. You call it whatever it is that will make you feel better, and not so small. The smell of the parking lot baking in the sun, like tar and banana peels: you call it grand. The coffee you're drinking—the best cafe latte you've ever had; the donut you're eating—a delicious apricot scone; the thing that you're doing (helping Nan pick out a prom dress)—fun. Whatever you do, you don't call it what it is because calling it what it is ("So, another one left you huh?") is Nan's job. She's five-nine, one hundred-twenty pounds, and she's about to ask you, "Do you think these pink leather pants make me look fat?"

Don't think.

Don't consider what's *really* happening.

Say, no.

Say, they don't.

Say, you're not fat.

Whatever you do, don't say what's on your mind, because what's on your mind could destroy someone like Nan—put her in therapy for years, make her buy a hideous prom dress.

"By the way"—*this is what you'll want to say*—"tell me again how it is that my boyfriend ended up sleeping with your best friend?" *(Remember, you're here to help with a prom dress.)*

"You don't look fat."

"I don't?"

This is perfectly acceptable dialogue between a niece and her aunt. This is only you and Nan, sweet Nan, not the high school sex kitten who gave your boyfriend head.

"I think I want a backless dress."

Forget.

Forget while you stand here, waiting for the mall to open, that you were dumped again, that you said, "This time it'll last." Forget how many times you've said that.

Pretend. Pretend that you're not angry at Nan for knowing the girl Sam left you for. Better yet, pretend that when you asked her about this girl, she didn't say, "Know her? We're like best friends."

Smile.

And tell her that the apricot scone is good, the café latte delicious, and the look of disbelief and disgust on your face is only fatigue. Say, "I'm exhausted," and smile again. Assure her it has nothing to do with Alyssa (cute name), Sam's new lover and Nan's best friend.

Go into the mall when it opens and continue to smile and pretend.

EARLIER

"It'll be good for you." My sister is baking cookies again.

"It'll be good for *you*," I say.

"She'd love it if you went." She's trying to talk me into going shopping with Nan.

"She'd love a hotel room for prom night—are you giving her that too?" I press my palms against my forehead.

I'm in Andrea's cream-colored kitchen (which happens to match the weave in her hair) and she's standing at the counter, spooning drops of dough onto a cookie sheet.

"I just think it'd be really good—"

"You already said that." I'm sitting at the yellow-flowered tile-top table trying not to notice how much weight Andrea has gained. "You do know Sam fucked her best friend?" I knew all this baking would catch up to her one day.

"Ally, you need to get out. Get some fresh air."

There's absolutely nothing in the World of Andrea that can't be fixed with a batch of homemade cookies or a breath of fresh air.

"We live in LA. There is no fresh air."

She waddles over to me (I'm exaggerating here—she's probably only put on five pounds), and drops a warm cookie onto a plate in front of me.

"Eat," she says.

And I do.

"How are they?"

"Good." They're always good. She entered the Betty Crocker Bake-Off when she was ten. 'A cookie-baking prodigy,' they said.

"So, what do you think?"

The night she won the Bake-Off, we went to Sambo's to celebrate.

"Nan would love it."

Sambo's had big booths and great sundaes. I ate the whipped cream off both our banana splits and threw up in the parking lot before my mother had time to yell at my drunk father for being two and half hours late. Our family really knew how to celebrate.

"Did you put raisins in these?" I say, and I watch Andrea spoon more cookie dough onto the warm cookie sheets. I see the dough melt around the edges instantly.

"You know"—Andrea breathes deep—"you can't keep meeting guys like this."

"Oh, yes I can." I finish off the rest of the cookie. "It's easy."

TEN TEN AM

"Nothing too slutty," Nan says.

I'm here to get some fresh air.

"I mean, I want something sexy, but nothing too *slutty.*"

I'm here because for two weeks (fifteen days, really), ever since Sam left, I haven't had any air, haven't even really taken a deep breath—I've just been holding it at bay at the base of my throat. As we move through the mall's wide aisles, the air is a cool seventy-two degrees. A homeostasis of artificial air. I can feel it like something physical, tangible, touchable—I can feel this air.

"And nothing red."

"No slutty red dresses," I say.

I breathe deep. I suck up gallons of artificial air.

TEN THIRTY-TWO AM

By now the mall is full and the air is thick with aromas of courtyard food. Hot dogs, pizza sauce, Chinese braised tofu, french fries and Rice Krispy squares. I'm not listening to Nan anymore ("not too this, not too that"). I'm breathing a smorgasbord of air and concentrating hard, trying not to imagine Sam fucking Alyssa in her drill team uniform. Trying not to picture them each time Nan says 'sexy,' 'slutty,' or 'not too red.'

"Janine Basset will be wearing red." We pass by the toy store. "I don't want to be caught dead in red."

Nan steps over a chained-up battery-powered pig and barking dog. "Oh, look," Nan says, pointing to a basket full of Magic 8-Balls. "I love these." She picks one up and shakes it. "They're so full of shit."

"You think magic is shit?"

"Will I find a perfect prom dress?" She holds it tight and turns it over.

YES.

She giggles. "Everyone knows it's not magic, more like, you know—that thing with The Edge."

"Coincidence."

"Yeah." She shakes again. "Will Mom let me get a hotel room on prom night?"

NOT LIKELY.

She laughs again.

"Here, you ask it something."

She hands me the Magic-8 Ball. I stare at it. It stares backs. The green toucan on the floor does a back flip.

A REVELATION IN THE MIDDLE OF THE MALL

Magic 8-Balls are cheaper than therapy.

Ask a question: one in eight chances, the answer you want will be the answer you get back. Who can beat that? Not even Vegas can give you odds like that. And so what if it's a coincidence, just an inexplicable occurrence—remember, you've become quite fond of coincidence and chance and things that are full of shit. In fact, you've always been fond of it, embraced it.

When I was twelve, I had a Ouija Board I would talk with. I'd ask it all kinds of questions: what's your favorite ice cream? What's your highest score on Centipede? Why does Mom look so sad? When's Dad coming back? Rocky or Bullwinkle—who do you like best? Never realizing the whole time I was disturbing the dead. I just liked having someone to talk with.

Suddenly I realize: I don't need Sam, I don't need anyone. I just need my Ouija board back, or perhaps a Magic 8-Ball—just someone to talk with. Tonight after the mall, after the dyed-to-match shoes, the cinnamon bun and cherry lemonade that I'm sure we'll have, I'm going to find my Ouija board, packed away with high school memorabilia—dried corsages and signed year books—and I'm going to try and contact Sam (though I know he's not dead). I'm going to ask him where he put the lid to the laundry detergent; at which dry-cleaners—the one on Ramon or Sunrise—did he drop off my favorite silk blouse; and why it is that I keep meeting men like him, men who, after a few months (once it was a little over a year) discover that I'm too needy, too clingy, too tall, too much in love with them.

"I hate this part," I said to Sam.

"What part?"

"The part where you tell me it's not me, it's you." I took a deep breath. "This part hurts like shit."

"Are you gonna ask it if Sam's coming back?" Nan is standing too close to me.

I drop the 8-Ball into the basket and kick the toucan. "Can we please just get you a prom dress?"

EVEN EARLIER

"I can't believe you're doing this *again*."

He said, "Again?" He was packing his things.

I asked, "Who is she?" He told me, "It doesn't matter." I said, "It *always* matters." He said, "Always?" "Tell me her name," I said.

That's when I began to suffocate.

His suitcase was so full, like a belly of sorts. He didn't even have this much stuff when he moved in—what could really be in there?

"I don't know why you're doing this." I was sitting on the edge of the bed.

"Because I'm leaving you." He moved closer to the suitcase, farther away from me.

"Don't bother trying to remember everything," I told him. "Chances are, when you leave you'll purposely forget something so you have to come back."

"I'm not coming back."

"You will. They all do."

"They?"

"Just tell me her name."

He took the suitcase off the bed.

"When you come back because you forgot your fucking toothbrush, knowing her name will make it harder to take you back."

"Alyssa," he shouted. Then he left.

DRESSING ROOM #10

Alyssa is eighteen (legal, Sam reminded me), blonde (he made sure to tell me) and really, really loves him (Nan informs me in the junior section of Nordstrom's.)

"And she studies horticulture," Nan yells from the dressing room.

"So?" I'm standing on a chair, trying to adjust a vent. My arms are above my head and I'm on the tips of my toes.

"So, Sam is into all that shit." Nan comes out in a full-length burgundy gown.

"He has a cactus garden."

"They talk about plants. She says he likes to talk about his plants."

"I'm not sure if cacti are plants." I can't get the air to come out the vent, I can't look at my niece in one more dress, I can't even believe for a moment that Sam is fucking Nan's best friend while they talk about plants.

"Whaddya you think?"

"Too slutty," I say. I hit the vent; I almost fall off the chair.

"Really?" Nan says.

"They're not plants." I suck air through the vent. "They're succulents."

On our way to the next dress shop, Nan gets Hot Dog on a Stick and asks me if I want one. I say no, no thank you, no Hot Dog on a Stick. And, as we're walking, she's talking and lots of people are stopping and she's saying this is my Aunt Ally, and this is so and so, and the so and so's are saying, "Oh!" and "Oh," like they know me. And pretty soon I'm convinced that the next one—the very next one—will be Alyssa in a Cinderella ball gown with Sam standing next to her in a tux and she'll have on an awful corsage, one with oversized daises and chrysanthemums, and replete with baby's breath, I bet. Because, regardless of what Nan says about his love for plants, Sam's taste in flowers stink. Hideous. Bought me purple carnations for my birthday. And for Chrissakes, I want to tell Nan, it was only a few cacti. I don't think it could even qualify as a garden, maybe a collection, but certainly not a garden. "I have two houseplants. Does that make me a fucking botanist?"

"What?" Nan has a mouth full of fried cornmeal and dog.

"You heard me."

She throws the stick into the trash. "Oh, will you just get over it?"

"Good hot dog?" I ask.

THREE NIGHTS AFTER SAM LEFT

I'm sitting in Andrea's kitchen, getting sick from her chocolate macadamia nut cookies and homemade butter pecan ice cream. I'm drunk with gluttony. The ice cream machine is spinning. It's noisy and I feel dizzy.

"I never should've sent him out for cigarettes."

"He didn't leave you over cigarettes, Ally." Andrea is spooning.

"Yeah," Nan says. "I mean, Alyssa smokes too." Nan just got through telling me how Alyssa met Sam. In a Circle K after the homecoming bonfire. "It was so romantic," Nan said. That was the night I sent him out for cigarettes.

"Isn't she too young to smoke?" Andrea makes a different recipe each time they leave me. Steve, who after two years went to Hawaii and never came back—his batch won a local contest. Caramel-Pecan Chocolate Chunk, or, Stevens.

"She's eighteen," Nan says, pouring more salt over the spinning ice cream machine.

"Yeah." I pull out a pack of cigarettes. "She can vote, smoke, and fuck my boyfriend legally." I light one, "She should definitely be prom queen."

"Don't smoke in here," Andrea says.

Nan takes her cookies and bowl of ice cream into the other room. "This has nothing to do with me," she says as she leaves.

"Why are you doing this?" Andrea begs, clicking off the noisy ice cream machine.

I flick ash in one of Andrea's antique teacups sitting on a cream-colored doily and pick up another cookie. "You know, Andrea"—I take a bite—"This may just be your best batch yet."

ONE HOT DOG ON A STICK, ONE ICE CREAM CONE, AND TWO FRESH SQUEEZED LEMONADES LATER

"So what do you do in horticulture class?"

We're in Macy's and we've tried on seventeen black dresses. Three were too small, two too big, and one, the zipper broke (Just put it back. Shouldn't we tell someone? You'll have to pay to have it fixed). Five "makes me look fat"; two "makes me look like death"; and four looked better on the rack.

"We look at plants." We now have on a blue dress.

"What kind of plants?"

"Green plants."

It's definitely time to decide on a dress. "I think I like this one best."

"Not too sexy?" Nan's looking in the mirror. She has a tattoo of a cricket on her calf and is wearing a toe ring.

"No," I say. I can't feel any air moving through me.

She turns around in the dress and there's no back. "Not too tight?"

"No." This may be where I faint from not taking a breath.

"Open-toed shoes or closed?" She takes off the dress. She's wearing a g-string and has a navel ring.

"Closed." The night he left, Sam mentioned something about Alyssa's tongue-piercing and oral sex.

"I think open."

"Then why the fuck did you ask?"

I try not to feel bad for what I just said, for the tears welling up in Nan's eyes, for the silver eyeliner running down her face, for all the times they left, for all the times I swore I wouldn't take them back. I try not to feel bad about that.

"What's wrong with you?" she says. Then she says, "What is *really* wrong with you?"

I try not to think about what she just asked. And I try to call the room spinning and me not breathing and a crying Nan standing half-naked with a hanger: coincidence. Chance.

"I'm going outside to get some fresh air."

"Enjoy your cigarette."

As I'm walking, I stop and look back. "When I asked what kind of plants, and you said green plants, I forgot to laugh." She slams the dressing room door on me. "That was funny, and I forgot to laugh."

OUTSIDE THE MALL

Okay, so maybe it was a garden. And maybe I never asked him about it. In fact, maybe, just maybe, I really knew how much he loved that garden and how much he hated that I never asked about it. Just maybe.

Just maybe I never noticed him standing in the bathroom late at night with a pair of tweezers, sitting on the toilet pulling thorns from his hands and thumbs. Maybe I never noticed the way he flinched with each tug of his skin, maybe I never saw happiness like that.

And maybe, just maybe, there was an awful lot we both never noticed. Like the way his voice got sloppy and loud when we would drink, or the way too much alcohol always made me cry and talk about my Dad. Or the way love in your thirties—is different from love in your twenties—because in your thirties, you realize this may be the best love you'll ever have.

And maybe I always knew Sam and I would never last, just like the rest, that he would never be fully mine, all mine—the same way you know an injured bird you rescue or a wild rabbit you catch will only stay with you until they can fly away or until you carelessly leave the cage door unlatched. Lots of things leave just because someone's careless with a latch.

Maybe I knew all that.

A LITTLE LATER

On the way home in the car, I try and figure out the title and artist to every song that comes on the pop radio station, just so I have something to ask Nan.

"Brittany Spears," I finally say.

Nan rolls her eyes and shakes her head. "Mom was right."

"About what?" These are the first words she says to me since the Macy's dressing room. She told the shoe salesman at Leed's I was a strange lady who was following her around the mall. She didn't want me to come back in the store until they wouldn't let her write a check and I had to pay cash.

"About you hating me over this."

"I don't hate you." I give the air conditioner an extra click.

"It's not my fault, you know." She looks out the window and, for the first time all day, she looks like Nan again. Small, tiny features, incredible ivory skin. "She happens to really love him."

"I'm sure she does." And the way the sun hits Nan's cheek through the window and the way the light makes her eyes squint, I am reminded of the summers we spent at the lake when she was nine. Putting sunscreen all over her skin and sitting under the open tent. "But I don't think she really loves him."

"I don't think you know what love is."

"Did your mother tell you that?"

She looks at me with disbelief. "What do you care anyway?" She looks out the window again. "You'll have another one in a few weeks."

"That's not fair."

She shakes her head, "No, that's just sad."

Each year, Nan was the only one who came home from the lake without a sunburn—just a really great tan.

THAT NIGHT

Toys 'R' Us doesn't carry Ouija boards anymore and I can't find mine. "Too many cults and satanic rituals with today's kids. Not like when we were young," the cashier says. "When we were young?" I say. The insecure paranoid stuff is already setting in.

I buy a Magic 8-Ball instead and remind myself about aging. About this phase of insecurity and worthlessness that doesn't usually settle in until week three, sometimes four, and, as the cashier counts me back my change, I get really pissed off at the prematurity of this stage.

The grieving process my therapist calls it. For one hundred and seventy-five dollars an hour, you would think by now she could tell me how to grieve guys like Sam completely out of my system. An absent father, an enabler mother, you grew up in the shadow of your sister—cheerleader, prom queen—you were a fat kid. "I lost all that weight my senior year." You have issues with food. "I have issues with the people I love fucking someone else." You're uncomfortable with your body in bed.

"Why do you continue to see her?" my sister asks.

"She's the only one who's there when they leave."

"I'm here."

"You're busy with Nan and Frank." (Her husband—they've been married for years.)

"You know what I think would be great?"

"What?"

"You should take Nan shopping for her prom dress."

I'm on my couch, I'm getting drunk, I'm taking inventory of all the things I've gained each time "they've" left. A lava lamp, a hat rack, a Foos-ball table, a blender (now I have two), and a cat.

"Don't take the cat."

"It's my cat," Charlie 1993 said.

"He likes me best."

This is how my relationships usually end. Someone fighting someone else for custody of the cat.

"Why does this keep happening to me?" The Magic 8-Ball is between my legs and the cat is on the coffee table trying to figure out how he can roll this big black globe off my lap.

I pour another glass of red wine. Sam hated red wine. And this is religious: doing whatever it is they hated until I am sick and polluted from the act. Watching *Riverdance* on video twenty-four times was by far the most tortuous.

"Is he coming back?" I pick the 8-Ball up. It's smooth and cold. One in eight chances, I think. I shake.

NO.

"Is it me?"

NO.

"If he does come home, will I take him back?"

YES.

"Figured that." I pour another glass and spill a little on our leather couch. Not "ours" really, more like mine; I bought it on my credit card. The drop rolls right off the edge. Sam promised to pay for half.

I turn the 8-Ball upside down and shake again. The water inside the ball is thick and blue. And now, it hits me like it always does. I am alone again, drunk again, with all the Ikea furniture and candle displays again.

"Will it always be like this?"

I stare at the cat.

I shake.

He looks confused.

I ask again, "Will it always be like this?"

I wait for the cat to answer back.

PROM DAY

I call and ask Andrea if I can come over and help Nan.

"Don't upset her, Ally."

"I won't."

"Have you heard from Sam?" is the first thing Nan asks me when I walk in.

"No."

Her room is full of steam from the bathroom and she's wrapped in a towel, painting her toenails. "Alyssa is really upset."

I grab the bottle from her and finish her pinky toe. Slate Blue. The color is dark, almost black.

"She thought she was going to prom with him."

I laugh.

"This isn't funny." Nan throws off her towel and pulls on her underwear. "No matter what you think, Alyssa is my friend." It's as if she's changing in gym class, as if I'm not even standing here. "She has her dress and everything."

"Nan." I don't think I can do this.

"We rented a limo." She pauses. "It has a moon roof and a full bar."

"Sam is thirty-two years old—why did she think he would go to the prom with her?"

"The same reason you thought he loved you, I guess." She rolls on deodorant. "Because that's what he said. Because that's what she wanted to believe."

It's unbearably quiet while she splashes something fruity and sweet on her skin.

For a long time, I sit and watch her dress. Pantyhose, earrings, something small and sparkly for her hair, a bracelet with rhinestones that matches her blue dress. And before I say what any Aunt should say, I take a long deep breath.

"What do you want me to do, Nan?"

She slips on her dress and smiles—one of those half-smile-half-cry things—and backs up to me. "Nothing," she grabs my hand. "Just zip." And I pull up the zipper to her dress.

When she turns around, I, too, am doing the half-smile-half-cry thing and perhaps it's because she's beautiful in her dress or perhaps it's because she's growing up so fast or perhaps it's because her mother (my sister) is standing in the doorway with a camera.

And I want to tell her that she looks incredible, and that Alyssa will be fine, and that I'll be okay—really okay—but most of all, I want to tell Nan, sweet Nan, that she'll be great. But instead I just look at her and say, "We sure picked out a hell of dress, didn't we?"

IN THE END

On the lawn outside Andrea's house, Frank poses with his daughter and calls her 'kitten.' Before the limo pulls up, before he starts to cry, he waves at me and goes inside.

"Big baby," Andrea says.

When Alyssa gets out of the limo, she's everything and nothing that I expected her to be. She's not as blonde, not as tan; she's smaller and looks smarter than I imagined. I can see she must really care about plants.

She's with the boy they call "The Edge." Nan looks at me and winks and says, "What a coincidence."

I wink back.

One in eight chances, when I get home Sam will be there as if he never left.

NORMAL ENOUGH

I visit my brother-in-law, James, my mouth sewn shut, in Riverside County Mental Health. I have a pack of cards to give him so he can play solitaire.

A routine wisdom tooth extraction gone wrong. They were impacted. Rooted so deep inside the bone, that when the doctor pulled a bit too hard, my jaw snapped in half. Waking up with wires in your mouth and an ice pack on your face, staring at a nurse who whispers a little too sweetly, "You'll be okay," really screws with your brain.

But I don't say this to James when I see him. Screw. Screwy. There are certain things, words and phrases, you just don't say to someone who's locked away in the crazy place. In fact, there's a whole list of words that are now off-limits in my husband's family: crazy, lost it, nuts ('cashew' and 'almonds' are okay—from now on, all nuts must be called by their formal names).

James tells me to be careful.

"Why?" I say. He's barefoot and wearing a white t-shirt and jeans.

We're sitting at a pink formica table pocked marked with cigarette burns in the middle of a very large room. Though large, there is nothing spacious about this place. There arc a few tables and various people sit at them alone. Some talk to themselves.

"With your mouth sewn up like that, they might think you're one of us." James shuffles the deck of cards in his hands.

The night of my wisdom teeth operation, I woke up thinking I was dead. I could hear my voice echo inside my head.

Somewhere in-between the nurse telling me I'd be okay and my waking up in the middle of the night to pee, James went crazy.

"And with the way you talk, your teeth all clenched up, you sound like me." James' tongue is swollen and he moves slowly because the medication is settling into his system. This is what Ralph, his social worker, tells him. "The settling is what makes him talk funny." We all like Ralph. He's a good guy and tells "Yo' mama so fat" jokes when he comes in at night.

"They just might keep you here." James looks at me as if begging for something. Understanding, compassion, maybe just a grin. And this look that is neither disturbing nor particularly sad, makes me think of his wife and baby. "It's not so bad in here," he says. "It's kinda okay, I guess."

When they hand out the cigarettes at four o'clock (six, eight, ten, noon, two, four, and then all over again) and open the door to the yard, the technician, in the blue uniform with teddy bears on it, hands me one. "Thank you," I say.

James and I laugh and go outside to smoke our cigarettes. It's quiet in the yard and, for a moment, neither one of us feels the need to fill up the silence between us with empty words.

"This is nice," I finally say, and James grabs my hand.

Once in a while I write things down. *Water. Vanilla Shake.* When it's late at night and my mouth aches: *Call my mother and tell her not to come here. Cup.*

"What for?" Marc asks.

A Big Cup, I write.

Each time I pass the pad of paper back to him, he looks at it inquisitively for a long time, even if it's just one word. It's as if he's trying to figure it out, read something other than what's really there.

"What do you want in it?" He starts to move from the couch to the kitchen sink, his hand reaching for the cupboard before he's even close to it. "This cup?" He's been like this ever since I woke up. Waiting on me like they sewed my legs together, not my jaw. "Cup? This cup? Coffee cup?" He's talking to me like pet-owners talk to their whining dogs: *Walk? Bone? Bone—you want a bone, girl?*

"I just want an empty cup." I sound like my mother, when, in the mall, she'd scold me and my brother through clenched teeth, angry and frightened that we'd run off.

"What for?"

"For James." I sound hard and bitter when I speak.

"What?" He's frustrated.

"For James."

He shakes his head, grabs the biggest cup he can find, and brings it over to me.

I write in big letters with three lines underneath it, *FOR JAMES*.

When he sees this, his whole body—from his eyebrows down through to his fingertips—deflates. I can see how loose and thin his skin is, how much he's aged.

He hands me the cup. His head slightly turned, tilted to one side. He hands me the cup without looking at me, as if he were making an illegal or immoral exchange.

Thank you for the cup, I write, but Marc has already walked away.

The day before my surgery, I had lunch with James at Coffee.com and we both ordered tuna fish sandwiches we didn't eat.

"I don't think that's a good idea."

James told me that he and Tara weren't happy, and that he wanted to leave.

"I don't think that's a good idea, with the baby and everything."

James and Tara have a nine month old, Elijah—plump and oblivious—and another on the way.

"I'm tired, Julie." He picked up his iced tea and moved it to the other side of the plate. "I'm just tired of everything." Without ever taking a sip, he picked it up and moved it back again.

I ask Marc to come to the hospital with me.

"I'm going to church." He's in the kitchen stirring his coffee.

"Church?" I'm getting good at forming words behind the curtains of my teeth. "You don't go to church."

"I do now."

"Is this your mother's idea?"

"What?" He's getting good at pretending he doesn't understand me.

I grab the pad of paper and pen by the phone. *Praying isn't going to make James sane.*

He reads it and throws his spoon in the sink. "Neither is bringing him a big cup and watching him play solitaire all day."

"He's your brother for Godsake."

"You don't have to remind me."

From the shower, I hear the garage door open and his car pull away. He's having a hard time with this. Not his wife's mouth being wired shut—that just irritates him—but for James being in there. 'This' and 'there' are synonyms for James' condition ('condition'—another synonym). I'm okay with this, I guess—the synonym part—because 'this' and 'there' are much easier to say than 'bi-polar,' 'mania' or 'institution,' even when your mouth isn't wired shut.

Church is where things got bad, where they finally decided to put James away. His mother thought Jesus might be able to help. This was the same night I woke up to pee. Marc was gone and I could hear my voice echo inside my head.

"Why would they even want to go back there?" James says to me on the phone when I call to tell him I'll be over to visit around noon.

"You know the way your mother thinks." I'm putting on make-up; the phone is clenched between my ear and shoulder.

"Tell her God's not going to save me."

"I told her."

"Tell her Nicholas Cage is."

Marc's mother says men have a harder time with things like this because they're not as strong. That, of course, is why women have babies.

"God's plan is a perfect one. Women were created to endure pain, to smile through anything." This is what she said before James started talking about Nicholas Cage. "Everything's going to be okay." Now it doesn't seem likely she'd even smile through a dancing pig routine.

She's thin and pretends she's sleeping regularly. But her nine-year old daughter, Jessica, says she can hear her crying all the time.

"She says God will get her through this." Jessica and I have Baskin-Robbins chocolate shakes on Wednesdays after her dance practice.

"What do you say?" When we talk, we don't pretend James isn't crazy. "Do you think God will save him?"

She points to my mouth. "Does that hurt?"

I shake my head and smile. "How's your shake?"

I'm walking out the door when my mother calls.

"Hi, honey."

I'm drinking a protein shake (I stopped putting berries in them because of complications with the seeds), I'm getting ready to leave, I'm regretting not having pretended that I was already gone.

"It's me—Mom." Then, as always, she says, "You don't have to say anything."

So I don't.

"I just wanted to see about things." 'Things' mean me, my mouth, Marc—but, most importantly now—James.

"You know Janet's friend Karen?"

Everyone has a friend of a friend who's just like James.

I pay her little attention. I put dishes away, play with the cat, figure out what I can blend into liquid. Cream of wheat is nice, all fruits are good, and I never would have guessed how thin peanut butter can get with added milk.

"Karen has to take medication for the rest of her life." (Ralph said this too.) "When she doesn't, she goes on these ravenous shopping sprees." She laughs. "But last Christmas she bought all of us brand new VCR's!"

You'd be surprised how little you listen when someone says you don't have to talk.

At the hospital, I hand James the cup.

"Thanks," he says, and goes to fill it up.

They have him on Lithium and Zoloft, with Prozac thrown in for good measure. Besides making his tongue swell to twice its size (parts of it actually spilling out the front of his mouth), the drugs make him thirsty. Real thirsty. Last visit, he could only get through a sentence or two before having to get up for a drink of water from the fountain. The water fountain is located in the living room, just left of the TV. Each time James went for a drink, the crazy people would yell at him, "You're blocking the TV!" Some of them practiced being clever, saying things like, "You make a better door than a window." Then they'd laugh. Crazy people don't laugh like normal people.

"How's your mouth?"
"Better."
"Thanks for the cup."
"You already said that."
"Oh."

We go on like this for a while, trying to talk like regular people. All the drooling and slurring aside, we understand each other. We both understand how careful we must be to talk about nothing at all. Visiting hours are only twice a day: from noon to one, and then from five to six. Sometimes they let it slide, a few minutes over, maybe fifteen. One time it was a full half-hour, which was nice.

"I called the studios again today."

I try not to react and take a sip from James' cup. Most of it spills onto my chin and dribbles down my chest.

"I know he's going to come, Julie, I know it."

He's talking about Nicholas Cage, again. The actor, yes, but more importantly, the actor who played a successful businessman zapped into a new life with a wife and two kids in the movie *The Family Man*.

"He's coming with the Ferrari as soon as he lands in LA."

This, in part, is why James is here. Because they say he's choosing to live in an alternate reality. James has a family. A wife and a baby. Tara, his wife, hasn't come to see him in over a week. She says she's angry.

"I just don't know why Cage isn't returning my calls." He looks down at the table. They didn't know each other very long. Just a few months before she got pregnant and they got married. She's been packing her things and taking them over to her aunt's place. Little by little. No one says anything.

"I saw Elijah yesterday." I try to change the subject because Ralph says it's best to talk to James in terms of this reality.

"Cage has kids."

"He was laughing and smiling and he…" I stop, because I didn't see Elijah yesterday, and making up stories for this reality isn't really reality at all. If we're going to make things up, I, like James, would much rather talk about a Ferrari and Nicholas Cage.

"What are their names?"

"Annie and Josh." James turned twenty last week. "I think those are good names." Last Tuesday. "Don't you?"

Ralph said these symptoms are common in young men James' age. Between the ages of eighteen and twenty-five especially. "What kind of symptoms?" I asked.

"Split-personality, Bi-polarity, Mania, Manic Depression." Ralph sounded excited while making this list.

"Those are good names," I say.

They gave him a cake in the crazy place and sang "For He's a Jolly Good Fellow" instead of "Happy Birthday" because no one could decide if "and many more" is really part of the Birthday song. James said it almost made him cry.

"He promised he'd come, Julie." He leans into me.

It was easier in the beginning. When I wasn't expected to say anything because the swelling was so bad.

"There's a lot of traffic in L.A., James." Now, the swelling has gone down.

He looks up at me.

"If he lands in L.A."—I take a deep breath that whistles through me. "There's a lot of traffic in LA and that's maybe why he's running late."

James smiles so wide, his face gets big.

"Okay?" I ask.

"Okay."

When I get home, it's late and Marc isn't speaking to me. He doesn't ask where I've been, what I did with my day. He knows I was with James, and this bothers him for all the reasons I understand and probably a million others he's too afraid to share with me.

I undress, put on my robe, and run the bath. Marc comes into the room and just raises his eyebrows at me. I look up at him and then he leaves. This type of communication started long before James went crazy, before my mouth was wired shut. It started before we stopped talking about important things, like whether or not to have kids, or to buy a new car (he just pulled up in it one day). It started even before that, really. Somewhere between the innocent breakdown of "take out the trash" and "I thought I told you that."

I remember that, when I was a kid, I'd go underwater in the pool and talk, listen to my underwater voice, and laugh. That's how my voice sounds inside my head all the time. In the bathtub, I wonder: if I go under, if I hold my breath and attempt to talk, will things be normal again?

While sitting in the tub, I'm suddenly regretful of everything—above all, I'm regretful I lit candles this particular night. Because, in the shadows, I remember when we'd sit in here together with bubbles up to our ears. I smell the scent of pear, that body wash he bought me in Santa Barbara last year, and I can't help but wonder: what went wrong? Did it happen while we were sleeping? When, lying side by side, we somehow managed to never touch one another? Did it happen slowly like that, almost unnoticeably? Or did it snap one day, like James' brain, when we were just too tired or too stubborn to hear it?

I soak a washcloth with water and wring it out over my face.

The hospital asks all of us questions. What did he do the Saturday before? What did he eat? Does he do drugs? A checklist of sorts that will lead them closer to a diagnosis or, rather, a conclusion of when the separation began.

"These things are usually brought on by stress," Ralph said. "When the brain is overloaded, emotionally or otherwise, it either shuts down or splits. His split."

We all nodded and imitated that universal look of concern—the one where you squint your eyes and wrinkle your forehead.

"Has he been under a lot of stress lately? Emotional or otherwise?"

We all turned and looked at Tara. And that was unfair. She was holding Elijah so tight to her chest, I wanted to tell her to let him go.

"We have a lot of bills," she said.

"That would explain Nicholas Cage."

We took this statement as truth, a diagnosis of his disease, as if dreaming of Nicholas Cage were a medical term—something you'd find in a big, expensive book.

"Well then, what would explain him standing naked atop a church, shoes in his hands?" This didn't come out of my mouth clearly, and everyone asked, "What?" Because they didn't understand, or because they didn't want to understand, or because the image of James, blonde and young, screaming from the rooftop, directing his family to take off their shoes—"Take off your shoes and you'll be grounded" was more than any of them could bear. "Grounded," he'd said. And even though I wasn't there, though I wasn't watching his body teeter on the edge of a building (I was lying in bed, doped up on Vicodin), I know this was more than even I could bear.

Marc knocks on the door. "Are you okay in there?"

Before I can answer, I think how strange it is for him to be too afraid to open the door, to see his wife naked in the bath.

"I'm okay," I finally say.

The next morning, the entire family meets with James. Except for Marc and Jessica.

We talk about James as if he isn't there. "James was a normal kid." As if he isn't in the room at all. "Good grades and a little bit of trouble in his senior year. He was raised in a house of God." This is what his mother tells Ralph, and Ralph laughs—then stops when he realizes how serious she is.

"That may be part of it," Ralph says. We all take a deep breath along with Ralph because we instinctively know what's coming next. "Was there a lot of pressure on him to be good, to do what was right all the time, to please you?"

And, again, we all look at Tara.

This time Tara doesn't say anything back, and, for the first time in a long time, I feel badly. A little guilty, maybe even a little ashamed.

"Listen, Ralph"—Marc's mother won't stand here and listen to this—"I'm not going to stand here and listen to this. To you telling me that I was a bad mother, that I did wrong by him." She straightens down the back of her hair with one hand and says, "Now, I think that what James needs here is a little prayer." And we all join hands.

This time, even Ralph pretends to pray.

After group, I visit with him. It's Movie Day. They all vote the night before. James says it isn't democratic at all—usually the craziest one wins.

"Leif likes me, so he mostly leaves me alone." We're smoking our issued cigarettes again. "His favorite movie is *Austin Powers*."

"One or two?"

"Two." He extinguishes his cigarette and tells me I'm getting pretty good at that.

"At what?"

"Talking through your teeth."

"James." I take a drag. "Do you know why you're here?"

"Do you?" The sunlight dances around in the yard, then behind the clouds. We fall in and out of its light seconds at a time.

I put my hand over my eyes. "I don't think you belong here." I try to move where I can see him clearly without squinting. "And they're making all kinds of decisions, decisions that you could make if you would just get better. I don't think you want to get better."

"It doesn't matter what you think. Or what I think. It matters what it looks like."

It's terribly hard to smoke a cigarette through my teeth and I start to choke.

"I may look crazy but I don't think I've ever felt more sane in my life." He pats my back twice. "Grounded."

I look down at his bare feet and take a deep breath.

"I'm not even tired any more. Remember how tired I used to be?"

"I remember."

Someone in the yard yells at Cinda, a regular who carries her birth certificate with her everywhere she goes. "Get the fuck away from me," they say. "Just get the fuck away."

We both turn toward the yelling, then turn away. "Are you going to finish that?" James points to my cigarette and I know we're through.

I hand it to him. "Tara moved out."

"I know." And he squints as the sun moves over us again.

"I don't think you look crazy." I watch him put his cigarette out on the ground and grab mine.

"No?"

"No."

He smiles. "Well, then I don't think you look sad."

In approximately two more minutes, the nurse will gather us in from the yard.

It's been three weeks since they broke my jaw, and the family has now decided to stop visiting James.

"What do you mean?"

"What?" Marc tells me this over dinner. Grilled halibut and brown rice for him, spinach and carrot juice for me. The cat is going crazy around Marc's leg, begging for a piece.

"I said, what do you—" I'm yelling through my teeth.

"I know what you said."

We do this still. Eat dinner together, even set the table.

"Julie, I don't want you going there anymore." He moves the food around on his plate and tries to ignore the cat wrapping and unwrapping itself around his leg. "They said that he's normal enough to go home. He just doesn't want to leave." Marc is growing impatient with the cat's howling.

"Normal enough?"

"Stop it, goddamnit." Marc drops his fork and it clatters against the side of his plate. It makes that startling kind of noise only a piece of silverware can make when dropped in frustration or anger. "I can't take it anymore." The cat darts a few feet away. "This isn't your charity case, this isn't a hobby—this is my brother. And when he gets out of there, when he wakes up and stops feeling sorry for himself, he's going to find out he's lost everything. Everything. And nothing will ever be the same." Marc picks up his plate and takes it to the kitchen. "You're not helping him." He pushes the cat away with his leg. "You're not going to save him. You have to stop seeing him." He leans against the sink. "Julie, please."

This is when I realize we aren't talking about James being crazy.

When they put you under for most dental procedures, you're in what they call a twilight sleep. Somewhere between waking and sleeping, as if you could be aware while dreaming—this is twilight sleep. Doped up on Valium, Nitrous oxide and Demerol. People can talk to you, and you can talk back, though you'll have little memory afterward. Of what you said.

I remember them saying 'we're almost through,' and thinking, 'I can't move.' My mouth and face were numb, my lips dry and cracked; I could taste blood. Then they put me in a little room. A nurse took my blood pressure what seemed much too frequently. I needed a driver. Marc got off work early. He sat there with me, inside the recovery room, and I tried to talk to him—there was something important I wanted to tell him. While staring at my spinach and carrot shake, with my husband leaning deep into the sink, I remember this: I had wanted to talk to him. And I remember crying, and then Marc crying, and then waking up alone in the middle of the night with voices echoing in my head. Meanwhile, Marc was busy trying to coax his kid brother off the edge of a building.

I look at Marc and then at the cat and, through my clenched teeth, I want to say sorry, or please forgive me. Instead I say, "Here kitty, kitty."

But the cat ignores me.

Later in bed I wait for Marc. We've never spent a night apart. Not in separate rooms, nor in separate beds. Neither of us has ever slept on the couch. We're proud of this. We talk about it with friends. "In all the years we've been married, I swear." Tonight will be no different. We'll lie in this bed together like we do every night, like we have for years.

I don't think I said anything interesting in the recovery room that day—nothing too revealing, nothing that Marc couldn't already see.

There was that time last Thanksgiving when we took a little too long cutting pumpkin pie in the kitchen. We could hear everyone asking, "Where have James and Julie run off to?" And then we heard Marc defending me. "She's a perfectionist when it comes to these things." And then Tara, over Elijah's newborn screams: "James probably appreciates that after being married to me." There were those long talks on the phone when Marc wasn't home. I would later tell

Marcs parts of the conversation. Marc would stop and ask, "You talked to my brother again?" Or there was the night I got drunk on sake and told Marc in the middle of a fight over recycling, "You'll never understand me like James does." And Marc said "what?" and I said "never mind," and we finished our California roll, paid our bill, and drove home without saying a word.

As I lie in bed, listening to Marc in the bathroom, I move my toes beneath the sheets and think about taking off my socks. I think about going barefoot and being grounded. Sane. But it's impossible. Marc is right about James, about James' condition, about a lot of things.

This, like everything—like Tara at her aunt's and Marc's mother praying to God and James in that cement room of the county hospital—is just another invented tragedy. We create circumstances just to carelessly muddle through them. They are harmless while they are happening, while we are busy skiing through the obstacles that distract us from our everyday, our bitterness, our should have's and wanted to's. They're no different than a new lover or a game of Nintendo. Novelties. And they only become real, become dangerous, when we want them to. And although there are many things I will never know about that night, I do know that James could have stood on the roof of that church until morning if he wanted to. There was no forcing him down.

He chose to be there. And I choose to be here, wondering if my husband'll ever be able to forgive me.

Marc shuts off the bathroom light and walks into the bedroom. I watch him move in the dark, and, although he's lived in this house for years—built parts of it himself even—he walks slowly, with outstretched hands, as if he's not familiar with any part of it.

"Good night," he says.

"Good night."

Dr. Siminiski asks me if I'm ready for this.

"I guess so," I say.

"What's the first thing you're going to eat?" His hands are large and he's snapping rubber gloves over them. The light on his head is shining in my face.

"Tuna."

"Tuna," he says, laughing a little like he cares.

"I like tuna."

When he starts clipping the wires off my teeth, little metal pieces go flying. Just particles and fractions of metal, but were one of those sharp little pieces of dust to find its way into someone's eye, the result would be disastrous. I close my eyes.

Dr. Siminski is still asking me about food. "How about a big juicy steak?"

"I don't eat red meat."

He continues to snip away.

James has a hearing tomorrow. A panel of physicians and psychiatrists. And Ralph will be there. They'll decide if he gets to go home or if he should stay in for fourteen more days. "It looks good," Ralph said, "especially since James was normal just a few weeks ago. I think we got this one early on."

"All done."

I open my eyes.

"How does it feel?" His hands are out of my mouth and the clippers are resting on my chest.

"Tight."

"It will be for a while. You haven't moved your jaw in over three weeks. Give it some time. Things should be back to normal."

"I know."

When he grabs the clippers from my chest and his big hands graze my breast, neither one of us says excuse me or sorry.

At home, I brush my teeth for the eleventh time.

"Feel good?" Marc says, sneaking up behind me.

"Clean."

"What's the first thing you're going to eat?"

We talk to each other's reflections in the mirror.

"Something crunchy." And I smile and Marc smiles and for a moment it's as if everything's okay.

"James gets out today."

"I know," I say. I wrap a long piece of dental floss around my finger. "What're you going to do?"

In the mirror, I slowly watch our smiles fade.

In James' hospital room, I watch him pack his things. The jury found him "not crazy enough" to harm himself or others. He hands me back the big cup.

"Thanks."

"No, problem," I say. His medication has settled in, and he'll be staying with a friend.

"How does it feel to have those things off your teeth?" He's shoving white t-shirts into a duffel bag and is standing barefoot. He catches me staring. "I threw away all my socks."

I smile and say, "It's weird. It's like everyone expects something wonderful to come out my mouth now. Like all this time I've been storing up words for them."

"I know what you mean."

He presses his feet into the linoleum; I watch him spread his toes.

"But I'm glad people can understand me again."

"I understood you."

He zips his bag.

"I know." I sit down on his bed. "I think that was always the problem."

"Julie, I'm sorr…"

"James." I stop him and we both look at the ground, his feet, the dusty baseboards.

"On top of that building, I felt so free. So uncomplicated. It was like I just woke up and realized how fucked up I had made things. I mean things were really fucked up, weren't they?"

"Yeah," I say.

"I'm not talking about you and me." He leans on the windowsill that doesn't have a window to belong to, just some plywood and chicken wire painted dark green. "I guess feeling that free makes you look crazy."

I laugh and twist the big cup in my hand.

"What's funny?"

"Feeling free doesn't make you look you crazy." The cup squeaks as I twist it. "You believing your buddy Nicholas Cage is bringing you a two-hundred thousand dollar car makes you look crazy."

James laughs, really laughs. Because his medication is now working and because he's going home and because he wants to fill the silence we now find uncomfortable. I laugh, too.

When it's quiet again, James looks out the window, through the plywood, as if he is admiring something out there, as if he can see a place past here.

"Is Marc with you?"

I shake my head.

"Tell him I'm sorry."

"I will."

And I press my feet through my shoes and try to feel the ground.

LOVE LIKE PRIMATES

The chimpanzees manifest intelligent behavior of the general kind familiar in human beings.
— Wolfgang Kohler; *The Mentality of Apes*

There are two messages on Stella's answering machine. One from her brother, the zoologist: "Hey, Janie, it's me. Bad news. Rosie died." And one from her husband, Peter: "Hey, Janie, it's me. I'm leaving." She takes down both messages as if they were the same and writes atop the Post-It pad: "Chimp dead. Husband leaving." Then she goes into the kitchen to get something to eat.

In the kitchen, Stella stands over the cracked grout of the counter and pretends to go over her lecture notes. *Chimpanzees show many emotional human traits in their "everyday" behavior.* She feeds herself stale saltines, one by one, until her mouth is full and dry and she can barely swallow. She doesn't go for water or a glass of milk—she keeps reading, ignoring the salty crumbs that fall first onto the yellow Post-It, then onto the lecture itself. *The chimpanzee's register of emotional expression is even greater than that of average human beings.* This combined effort—reading while consciously ignoring—is strenuous on Stella's eyes. Her eyes begin to blur and water, and parts of her body, its corners and bends, quiver and twitch. *The chimpanzee's whole body becomes agitated, not merely the facial muscles as in a human.* Stella breathes deeply and reassures herself while she reads: this is normal. This is not the end. This is just one dead chimp on a Post-It note. These are not tears. *Chimpanzees understand expression of subjective moods and emotional states in quite the human sense of the term.* "Chimp Dead. Husband Leaving." *Perhaps in even a greater sense than that of human beings.* Only the saltines are crumbling.

Stella wasn't the only one who expected the chimp to pull through. "Don't get hysterical. I know it's a surprise" was the rest of John's message on the machine. Rosie was doing so well last week. Picking up sweet yams with her hands and sucking on them. Everything pointed to the upswing. 'She seems to be doing so well. Yes, she's doing much better' was all the talk around the zoo. But Stella should have known: this is how things usually happen. Just when you think you have it figured out, it turns on you, vicious and relentless. The yams were nothing more than instinct. Like Peter waking

LOVE LIKE PRIMATES

in the morning and kissing Stella on the cheek—didn't mean he wasn't leaving. That's the problem with instincts, Stella thinks, her mouth thick and bumpy from the saltines: whenever we don't look for signs, we miss the neon ones right in front of us, the ones that stare us down and keep us up at night. Their blinking somehow penetrating our lids but we still don't see them.

Stella goes through the mail, tossing two coupons and a phone bill she had Peter pay online last week. She begins stacking and cleaning. Grocery list, lecture, newspaper, National Geographics, Post-It. *Under the influence of strong, dissatisfied emotion, the chimp must do something in the spatial direction of his emotion's object.* She knows the words by heart. "Chimp dead. Husband leaving." The way anyone would know something they've spent so much time on, dedicated a part of themselves so whole-heartedly to. *He must somehow get into touch with this projective, even if it's only to hurl the movables in his cage towards it.* She shuffles and restacks, shuffles and restacks as if the organizing will explain something. As if explanations explain anything. She tosses the stack, sans Post-It, into the trash that Peter would've taken out this evening.

Rosie became what the zoo likes to call 'a concern' about four months ago. Born and bred in captivity, she was passive and melancholy, often refusing food. She neglected her babies, leaving the zookeepers to mother them with diapers and teething rings. Rosie had beautiful babies but was never interested in them. The zoological society then decided to breed her with a new chimpanzee. Rocko was eager and aggressive—zoo language for a real son of a bitch with a mean right hook. Rosie loved him anyway. She followed him around their natural-environment cage. Often, she'd spend hours picking through his fur while he fingered, licked, or tried to mount another chimp. "This is typical chimp behavior," John had told her. "He'll come around," he said.

With Rosie dead and the lecture in the can, Stella thinks about cooking. Meatloaf or potatoes—something hearty. She takes out one pound of frozen ground beef and sets it in the sink. She stares, not sure what to do. Sauté it first with garlic and sweet onions, add green pepper and tomatoes, cover it with a dozen saltines and the caramel-soy latte she half-drank on the way home from teaching. Chimp Dead. Husband Leaving. This, and the echoes of lecture notes, are all Stella can hear while vomiting into the sink.

The lecture was to be given to a hundred eager freshmen on Monday—or at least that was the plan. "Expect to be here the entire class period," Stella had said.

Plans, like explanations, Stella realizes, mean nothing. Stella had planned to finish her lecture; Peter had planned to finish the outdoor sprinklers and watch the football game on Sunday; they had planned to make love every Friday. Stella had also made plans to visit Rosie on Monday, have coffee with her brother in the evening, call her mother on her birthday, and travel to Hawaii with Peter in the spring. She'd even planned—this weekend in fact—to tell Peter to ignore the sprinkler system out back. It wasn't that important to her. He could just rest and watch the game instead. Now, Stella's plans are reduced to getting up off the kitchen floor, stopping the nausea and the vomiting and the voices in her head, and seeing if it is at all possible to salvage the one pound of frozen lean ground beef defrosting and bleeding in the sink. *The crude stupidities of the chimpanzees may be mistaken as proof that the chimpanzees perform senseless actions, but toward apparent solutions.* Plans are only a suggestion of permanency. A shadow of something real, Stella thinks.

Stella's lecture birthed out of an on-going argument between her and her brother.

"They're not like us," he preached.

"Ninety-seven percent of the same DNA has to mean something, John." (This had been going on since they were kids.) "It's more than just a little facial hair." They both loved animals when they were young. They memorized Wildlife cards; studied genus, phylum, and species (Stella can still call any animal on the Discovery Channel by its scientific name); created animal clubs and an animal university; they even had their own zoo: thirteen rabbits, three dogs, two turtles, five cats, an aviary full of birds, and a voiceless rooster named Randy. All for the low, low price of a buck-fifty (just about what Stella paid for the cheap wine she's now drinking).

"DNA, yes," John had said. "But emotions—that's different. They're not like us emotionally."

"That's bullshit," Stella said.

"That's facts," John said. "Plain and simple."

John is now a Great Ape Specialist and head curator of the San Diego Zoo. Stella laughed at this title for years—she even made fun of it recently over Easter's honey-baked ham.

"Don't humanize them," he warned. "I worry that your lecture will be misleading."

"I'm referencing Kohler's work," Stella said. "Peter, tell him I'm referencing Kohler's work." But Peter was preoccupied, busily trimming every last stitch of fat—every last rubbery thread—off his slice of ham. Stella will remember this detail while grieving on the kitchen floor with a half-drunk bottle of wine, this sign that she had subconsciously dismissed.

"I don't believe in Kohler's work," John said.

Stella had ignored Peter's trimming deliberately, refusing to see it as some signal he was emitting, some infidelity pheromone she couldn't smell.

"Kohler is anthropomorphic," John said.

She will remember staring long and hard at Peter, at his discarded pile of fat.

"Kohler is an expert," Stella said.

She'll remember now how his collar was bent upward and seeming to press against his jugular.

"Don't you agree?" John asked, turning to Peter. Peter adjusted his collar away from the vein and said, "There's too much fat on this for me."

At a quarter to six, with the meat still rotting in the sink, Stella opens another bottle of wine and toasts Kohler three times. "Here's to the chimps," she says. "To their 3% of diversified DNA. To the chemistry of their bodies" she's mechanically prodigious in this state—"the quality of their blood, the quality of their most highly-developed organ: the brain. Here's to Peter and..." She stops, suddenly recalling that Easter Sunday.

"And to..."

And she doesn't know what to say. Her mind is both completely blank and completely cluttered. Peter refusing wine; Peter picking at deviled eggs; Peter with that ham; and then Peter, at Christmastime, sucking on one candy cane until it was white and thin. The other night, Peter rolled away from her in his sleep—seemingly automatic—when she brushed up against his skin. *The chimpanzee commits three kinds of human errors.* She remembers just then, with the empty glass in her hand, that she hadn't heard Peter pretend to laugh in years. *Error #1: Good Errors. The chimpanzee does not make a stupid, rather an almost favorable, impression, yet it is in complete juxtaposition to what the situation calls for.* Stella finishes off the wine and digs through the trash for her lecture.

John, and most of the keepers, were surprised to discover that Rosie had become pregnant. Most of Rocco's time, after all, was spent with other chimpanzees. One day, John jokingly said to Stella: "It just goes to show you never know what goes on inside of a couple's cage." This time, Rosie clung to her baby. She held it from the time it was born, tight to her chest, day and night. Carried it bundled beneath her arm like a football—like a real mom would. She stroked its tiny head and held it close to her mouth, giving it kisses and sweet yams strained like baby food through her teeth.

Upon recognizing the smell, they knew something was wrong. Rosie's baby; crib death. Still and silent. It took John and three other keepers eight days and one horrendous twelve-hour standoff to get the infant away from her. With the baby rotted and decaying, the mother, too, was infested with fleas and disease. "Primates do this in the wild, mostly."

John was clinical and serious because he had to be (though he mentioned that he hadn't slept a wink in weeks).

"Why?"

"Because it was hers. Alive or dead, when a chimp bonds, it's for good. We hold onto things. Why shouldn't they?"

"We hold onto things. Not dead babies. Besides, you're the one who doesn't believe in chimps' emotions."

He had to sedate Rosie just to pry the baby loose.

"Rosie had to have felt something." Stella stared at the baby's tiny body. "She had to."

He nodded and fluffed the baby's fur that Rosie's five fingers had matted. With just a few tears in his eyes, he said, "Stop reading in-between the lines, Stella."

At nine-thirty, in the dark kitchen, holding her lecture tight, Stella stares at the flashing light of the machine. She thinks about calling Peter and she thinks about this business of leaving. This business of finding and fucking. *The sexuality of these animals is fairly diffuse: there is no absolute orientation or differentiation according to sex.* And she thinks how willing she would be were Peter to have his way this time. This time, his way would be easy—less complicated than the times before. Dividing up CD's, arguing over furniture, putting his name back on the phone bill whenever he decides to return. His way is easier and more humane, Stella thinks, than explaining to Verizon that, yes, yes, he did move back in. Yes, again. *Error #2: Errors caused by complete lack of comprehension of a particular task's condition.* Yes, this time she would let him have his chimp and fuck it too.

"Peter took everything." Stella finds someone to talk to at midnight.

"So? They're just things." Sandy is also an instructor at the university. "Who gives a shit about things?" Stella could always count on a midnight phone call with Sandy, a horrible insomniac with a penchant for drink. Stella needs to count on this one—if only this one—consistency.

"Not just his things." *The meaning of things to chimpanzees can clearly be seen in the circumstances and behavior of the animals.* "The camera, the fish tank, his collection of CD's, sure—but other things, too." *Chimpanzees exchange and decorate one another with widely different objects.*

"What other things."

"Menial things." *A rope, a bit of rag, a blade of grass, a twig.* "The coffee grinder, the sugar bowl shaped like a turkey I use on Thanksgiving, the cartoon on the fridge I cut out last week." Standing in the bedroom, staring at a bare mattress stained from years of sleep, Stella thinks: this is very uncharacteristic of Peter. "He even took the sheets." Stella asks, "What does this mean?"

"It doesn't mean anything," Sandy says. *It means they play, not only with the things they have hanging round themselves, but, as a rule, with other animals as well.*

"You know how generous he is when he leaves. He never takes anything."

"Was." Sandy takes a sip of her scotch. "How generous he was. You gotta get used to the past tense." She takes another sip. Stella knows she's drinking scotch because she always drinks scotch—neat. Sandy's mother told her when she was five, "A woman is always a lady if she drinks scotch." Sandy's mother stopped drinking scotch in '75 when she discovered cocaine, and, because they don't let you bring scotch or coke into prison, she said she never really felt like a lady behind bars.

"I don't even know where he is."

"He's with the blonde—the one half his age—in the AmeriSuites down the street." She lights a cigarette and Stella can smell this too. "It's clichéd, yes"—she exhales, blowing out the match—"but it's classier than the Motel 6 with the coin operated bed."

Stella is spinning her finger around the edge of the wine glass, but it doesn't even make a squeak. "This sucks." Her mother had refused to buy them real crystal for their wedding. Said it was a waste. Instead, she gave them a glass frog ashtray that Stella broke against the wall above Peter's head on their third anniversary.

"Oh, Christ."

"What?"

"That silence."

"What silence?"

"You're about to say, you didn't see this coming." Sandy's phone voice is more authoritative and hostile than her real voice. "It's always, 'this sucks,' and then, 'I didn't see it coming.' Tell me you're not about to say you didn't see this coming?"

"I didn't."

"You did."

"Not this time." And now Stella is crying. "I didn't see it this time."

Sandy sighs deeply. "Change the subject." She finishes the last of her scotch. "How's the chimp?"

"Dead."

Sandy pours another.

"Died yesterday."

"Dammit." And they're both quiet. For longer than is comfortable. Just breathing and the clinking of ice cubes and the sound of cheap wine in an even cheaper glass.

"You'll be okay," Sandy finally says. "They're just things." Clink, clink. "Just fucking things."

At 1:30 a.m., Stella decides it's officially too late to call John back. She lies down on top of the Kohler lecture and prays for a good blackout. The kind that requires a briefing from a friend the next day. The kind that her mother said her father was in throughout their twenty-two years of marriage. The kind that makes Stella forget that, each time Peter leaves, she swears to never take him back. A real doozy of a blackout like that.

When John calls in the morning, Stella doesn't answer. She can't. In the daylight, without the wine, still sleeping on the naked bed, she can't bear to hear the details of Rosie's death. She rolls over and observes the enormous space on the mattress.

"Hey, Stella, it's me."

Stella knows her attachment to Rosie is strange. "Unhealthy," her brother once said. "But then again," he continued, "You've always gotten way too attached to things."

He said 'things' like one would say 'people.' He said 'things' in much the same manner as Peter, or Dad. She knew he even referred to himself as one of her 'things'. *The necessity of a group connection among chimpanzees is a very real force, of sometimes astonishing degree.* Celeste, John's ex-wife, also agreed. She called Stella "clinging" and "overbearing." *This is simply because the behavior of a chimpanzee's comrades constitutes the only adequate incentive for bringing about a great variety of essential forms of behaviour.*

"Stella, are you there? Pick up." John's message on the machine says that Rosie died in her sleep. "Don't want to tell you all the details on this damn thing, but thought you would want to know, y'know, about Rosie. Call me."

Beep.

What a beautiful sound, Stella thinks. "What a beautiful way to go, Rosie."

At Cal Poly Pomona, where Stella attended college, Dr. Zimmer told his zoology students the following. "People don't want to hear how animals in captivity really die, how gruesome and painful it is. Always tell them that they went peacefully in their sleep." Dr. Zimmer told Stella other things, too, like: "a female hyena (Parahyaena brunnea) has a mock penis," or, "the porcupine (Erethizon dorsatum) has a nose shaped like a man's prostate." Students didn't ask a lot of questions in Dr. Zimmer's class. Just safe things like, 'should we be taking notes,' or, 'is this going to be on the test?'

"No, it's fine if you come over." Sandy with the phone cigarette again. "But don't you want to wait for his call?"

"He's not going to call." Stella drives up University and turns on Mission Street, toward the park.

"He always calls. He'll call. There are arrangements to be made, things to be discussed."

"Like what?" She brakes for a kid on a ridiculous scooter and looks in her rearview mirror as if someone might be following.

"You're not very good at this, are you?"

"Should I be?"

"Well…" Stella hears a pause as she pulls into Sandy's driveway.

"But this is the first time that he's taken everything."

"Scotch?"

"Please."

Chimpanzees greet each other ritualistically with all degrees of emphasis and fervor, partly as reassurance of their social cohesion…

"How's the lecture coming?"

"It's toast."

"A double then."

"Please."

… but also as consolation in moments of terror and anxiety.

Sandy's house is "Old Beach," an actual type of real estate in San Diego. Hardwood floors with detailed baseboards and ornamental door handles that usually lock you out of the bathroom right when you have to pee.

"So now it's a formality?"

She hands Stella her scotch and they both sip and breathe.

Sandy teaches Poetry. She is still pretty and animated, even though twenty-five years of teaching and drinking, the hope that protesting in the 60's we're actually going to change things, a mother in prison, a dead father with a bloated liver, and two marriages have robbed the spark—the life—right out of her eyes. They're hollow and dark when she speaks.—as if she has just been rudely awoken from a dream.

"Are you wearing your clothes from Friday?"

"John said she died in her sleep."

"Oh, they always say that. That's bullshit." She tucks her linen skirt in-between her thighs and sits cross-legged on the couch next to Stella. "Like they're ever going to tell you they screamed all night, they begged for their life, they pissed and shit all over themselves when their soul finally left."

"John says animals don't have souls."

"Whatever. It's all the same." She takes another sip of her scotch, which she passes off as some holistic cider in her thermos in class, and stares at Stella.

"What?" Her face shows everything. The wine, the phone messages, the lack of sleep.

"Who is she this time?"

"Does it even matter?"

"It will in a couple of days."

"You know, all I hope—" Stella leans forward and puts her glass down on top of a *New Yorker* from last spring—"is that she's better than me. Smarter, prettier—just something."

"She will be. Tits two times the size of yours and she'll skydive or something."

"Do you think I'm hysterical?"

"We're all hysterical. Who said you were hysterical?"

"John and Peter." She picks up her drink again. "John, when he called about the chimp. 'Don't get hysterical on me,' he said. And then Peter last Christmas when I accused him of fucking Gina from the restaurant."

"Was he?"

"Of course."

"Then you're not hysterical. If you were blonde, half his age, with tits twice as big as yours, and you accused him of fucking the waitress, you'd be intuitive, not hysterical."

Stella lets out a small sound. Neither a laugh nor a cry.

"Go ahead," Sandy says, placing a hand on Stella's shoulder. "Go ahead, baby."

When Stella gets home, there's a message from Peter. "We need to meet for dinner to talk about things."

Beep.

Beep.

Beep.

"I need to get rid of this fucking machine." Stella hits delete.

At dinner, Stella tells Peter about Rosie.

"She seemed fine last week." He orders a vodka tonic from the waitress and smiles at her. *New female chimpanzees at once arouse the greatest interest on the part of the oldest, most dominate male chimpanzee.* Tony's House of Pasta is their usual meeting place.

"That was just a picture. What they show on TV isn't reality. It's what people want to see," Stella says as she tries to drown out the words in her head with the words coming out of her mouth. The waitress brings back Peter's drink and sets it on the table with a splash. "Oops," she giggles. Peter smiles, "It's okay." *The male chimpanzee immediately begins to busy himself with her in his most diligent manner, with sparkling eyes and a friendly demeanor.* The waitress giggles again. *Until at last she gives way to his invitations of play, to his embraces, and—rather shyly—to his childish sexual advances.*

"Stop doing that," Stella says.

"What?"

"This." Stella smiles at the waitress too politely. Almost instinctively, the waitress knows to walk away. "Did you have to take everything?" Surprisingly, Stella's voice is motherly and irritating, not sad and desperate like she wanted it to be.

"This isn't about things, Stella." Peter smiles at couples passing by as if searching for allies among the staff and patrons of Tony's House of Pasta.

"Oh don't do this, Peter. Don't tell me this isn't about things. Or if I say sex, say this isn't about sex. Or if I say love…"

"I love her."

Stella looks at him for a moment, then says, "No you don't."

"I do. I love her, Stella."

"Are you folks ready to order?"

From behind the wine menu that she hasn't been reading for the past ten minutes, Stella asks, "Does she love you?" *Error #3: Crude stupidities arising from habit.*

"Yes."

"Do you need some more time?" the waitress asks.

"Then I feel sorry for her," Stella says. *These mistakes occur in familiar situations, which the animal ought to be able to survey.*

Peter stares at her and asks, "Are you ordering the Caesar Salad?"

Such behaviour is extremely annoying to watch—it almost makes one angry.

"I'm not ordering anything."

Stella eats the Caesar Salad Peter orders for her. She knows the routine. Though each time she's here, she can't believe it. She's surprised to be eating anchovies and parmesan cheese.

"Ya know, you're just like him." The romaine is wilted and heavy with dressing.

Peter says nothing. He keeps his mouth so full of minestrone that she imagines him choking. "He does, however, have you beat." One green bean gone sideways—it would be the end of him, she thinks. "You're young, though. Four more in ten years should be a real walk in the park for you, Peter." She breaks a crouton with her fork. Stale breadcrumbs scatter across the table. "You've got my dad beat, easy."

By the time the entrées come, with Peter having said nothing other than, "I love her, Stella, I really do," Stella cracks another breadstick. She's concerned that this time just might be for real. This might be for sure. In four times, four Caesar Salads and four boxed eggplant Parmesans, Peter's done a lot of things. But one thing he's never done is take everything.

By the time Stella finishes the half-carafe of house Merlot and orders the crème brulee, she's making a scene.

"Don't make a scene." He has the entire wait staff at the House of Pasta smiling.

The group as a whole reacts so strongly on specially impressive, affective occasions. The group is a vaguely organized community of chimpanzees with a common interest. Stella pulls her chair closer to the table, catches the tablecloth on her high heels and spills her drink. Coffee and Frangelica run down her leg. "Shit."

"I don't think we should do this here." *Thus demonstrating their real human need for companionship and alliance.* Peter is mopping up the coffee with a linen, but it's not absorbing anything. He's pushing coffee around the table frantically. "I don't think it was such a good idea to meet here."

"But we always meet here." People are staring—the group is staring. "Oh right, but this time it's different. This time you love her."

"Stella." He puts the napkin in the center of the table when the crème brulee comes and smiles less convincingly. "I think you're upset about Rosie."

"That's funny." Stella cracks the sugar crust with the back of her spoon. "I think I'm upset because you're in love with the blonde you're fucking."

"She's not blonde."

"It's the artist from the faculty party, isn't it?"

"How's the crème brulee?" The waitress is back. *The newcomer is often a small weak creature who at no time shows the slightest wish for a fight.*

"Delicious," Peter says.

"So, I can start moving things?" Another blow to the dessert.

"What do you mean?" He's moved the linen and placed it over the coffee stain.

"Pardon," the waitress says.

"I'm the one leaving."

"Excuse me?" she says again. *The newcomer within the group will often utter the ape cry of indignant fury, which is at once taken up by others in the group as frenzied excitement.*

"He's not talking to you fuckface." Crack. The crème brulee is defenseless. The newcomer slightly wounded.

"I'm sorry," Peter says as the waitress walks away.

"That's rich," Stella says.

"The crème brulee," Peter asks.

"The fact that you can sincerely apologize to a total stranger."

"I'll get the rest of my things in a few days."

"That's good," Stella is through with the dissection of her dessert. "I wanted to be sure before I really started rearranging things, like last May. Moving the bedroom around, taking advantage of all that closet space."

"You can move anything you want."

"Okay, that's great. Because I have plans for the spare room. All kinds of ideas."

Peter throws a hundred on the table and says, "I'm leaving."

"I thought we already covered that."

Before he walks away, he gets quiet and turns to her. They both finally look at one another, and it feels foreign and strange. *The particular degree of friendship existing between chimpanzees at any one given time has special significance.*

"Was it bad? Rosie?"

Especially when there is a question whether a chimpanzee, while begging for something from another, will get it or not.

Stella stares at him long and hard. As hard and long as you can stare at a man you've been married to for twelve years and had four break-up Italian dinners with. "Of course not." *And, as a matter of fact, one will wait in vain for such kindness, when there is any coolness between the two animals.* "She went peacefully in her sleep."

"That's good," he says.

Nobody could look more undisturbed, more indifferent, more uninterested, than a chimpanzee from whom, with outstretched hands and pleasing voice, another is begging for food.

And Stella says, "Good." Then Peter walks away and Stella looks back at him while saying a prayer for the crème brulee.

It's almost midnight when Stella gets to the zoo. There's parmesan cheese stuck to her face. "I'm glad we're doing this on a Sunday." John points to the cheese. "The media'll be all over here tomorrow." She brushes her lip. "Dinner at the House of Pasta again?"

"Yeah."

They walk through the zoo in the dark. There's nothing to say and Stella still has parmesan cheese stuck to her face. "They just ran that special on Friday. Rosie playing in the exhibit, Rosie eating."

"Yeah, I know." We turn down Gorilla Lane. "Even Peter mentioned it."

"And how'd that go?"

"I told him she went peacefully in her sleep."

John nods his head and says, "This way."

Nighttime at the zoo is eerie and haunting. There are few lights that line the pathways. All the animals are locked away in their exhibits; the trees blow in the breeze, but the sound of the leaves blowing sound rehearsed—almost mechanical.

They get to the chimp exhibit *(Pan troglodytes)* and the moon hovers suspiciously over the tree where Rosie used to sleep. "We shouldn't have isolated her—" John turns the large crank on the cage—"but a catatonic chimp mourning her baby and affecting the group camaraderie makes for really shitty TV."

"You ran the footage from last spring?"

"Yep."

"The one with the tire swing."

"Yep." John stares into the cage.

"That's a good one," Stella says, and, for the first time since the two phone calls on Friday, Stella isn't confused about the pang in her heart—whether it's for Rosie or for Peter leaving.

The back gate to the exhibit slides open. Before they walk in, they're still for a moment. The darkness, the cement, the cold—Stella is reminded of a midnight conversation she had with John a few years ago, while standing huddled in a poorly-lit parking lot. "Stella," he'd said, "You married our father."

And now: "Who is she this time?" The familiar sense of naked honesty. "The chick from the faculty meeting?"

"How did she really die, Grape Ape?"

He looks down at his shoes and sighs. "I told you." *It is difficult to describe the methods of inter-communication among these animals.* He gently nudges her foot. "Still working on the lecture?"

She nudges back. *But among themselves the chimpanzees understand perfectly.* "Can't get it out of my head."

Inside the exhibit, there are rows of cages. The cage bars cast shadows onto the wet cement. They walk through this moonlit prison into the last cage Rosie occupied. They find her packed in dry ice, her body already bloated with chemicals.

"Are you sure everyone's okay with this?" Stella asks, stepping into the cage.

"They want a necropsy anyway." John leans against the cage door, his body tall and slim. "You've done it before."

Stella looks down at Rosie. Rosie's eyes are closed; her hands clasped over her big furry belly.

"Never on an ape." She places her hand over Rosie's. Rosie's hand is black, leather-like, and much bigger than Stella's. In a way, though, they're the same. Stella stares at Rosie's hand in awe, as a mother would stare at her infant's curled fist.

John steps in and tugs her elbow. "Wear gloves."

The two of them stand in the dark. His hand still rests on the point of her elbow; her hand hovers over Rosie's. They feel small again. Ten and twelve. Begging their dad to stop, to leave them alone, to just leave them alone. Begging their mom to never take him back. *Many chimpanzees will, in a bad mood, intentionally incite a mass attack; they'll fly into a rage over a trifle, and behave viciously in order to incite the herd.* "Please don't," they pleaded. Their mother promised, their father left, but on Stella's thirteenth birthday her father hit her so hard he cracked her jaw. "Happy Birthday," he said before raising his hand. The spit from her mouth blew out the candles on her birthday cake. *Thus, in a fit of anger, which the innocent observer had nothing to do with, the chimpanzee will attack him with fury.*

"What's that smell?" Stella asks.

"Going peacefully," John replies.

When doctors—specifically surgeons—say that after a while it's just a job, just a thing they do like pumping gas or bagging groceries, they're lying. A gaping wound never becomes an object or an organ, just a piece of meat. Handling Rosie's things isn't like a trip to the butcher—a liver, a kidney, a rump roast, a spleen—at least not for Stella.

She holds Rosie's hand. *Chimpanzee's large and powerful hands are natural links between themselves and the world of things.* Something deep inside Stella aches.

Rosie looks as if she's sleeping, like most large animals on the necropsy table. She's resting on the limb of a tree, her big fatty eyelids closed; she's not waiting anxiously to be put back together, to be stitched up, to be fixed. Smaller animals, like the armadillo Stella necropsied last spring, look lifeless and decayed by the time they get to the table. Rosie's body looks too big to have all life removed from it. Stella is careful. *Embracing or hand-clasping among chimpanzees is rare.* She moves things gingerly. *Yet when it is used, it appears as a spontaneous expression of joy or deep sympathy.* The whole time she never lets go of Rosie's hand.

Rosie's heart seems more alive than Stella's own heart. More animate, pulsing even. When Stella stares, though, she clearly sees that it's not beating, not pulsating; it isn't taking blood in, pushing blood out. It's weighty and flat. *Objects that are interesting to the chimpanzee, but unpleasant to handle, are approached, not with their hands, but by means of a stick.* Stella picks up a scalpel and pokes, lovingly, at Rosie's heart.

The necropsy report is normal. Except for all the damage to her brain.

"Why didn't you tell me?" Stella moves the phone to her right ear and lights a cigarette. She always picks up smoking when he leaves. One time, she got up to a pack and half a day before he called to say he missed her.

"We weren't sure."

"You didn't want to tell me." She inhales deep.

"What time is it?" John asks.

"Late." Stella hates the taste of cigarettes. "1:30 if I had to guess."

"Put the lecture down and go to bed."

"I can't." She watches the cigarette burn. "I can't."

Noraki and Katuya are brother and sister. They sit in the front row of lecture hall 204. They—foreign exchange students from Japan—have been there since last fall. They've been in Stella's classroom since Anthropology 101 began, every Monday and Wednesday for a total of sixteen weeks. *Chimpanzees very astonishing conduct towards a familiar human can be quite equivocal.* Today Stella stares at them as if she had never seen them before. She studies their faces, the subtle slopes of their nose, the flat fat behind their eyes. *There is no need for chimpanzees to know the human at all to be truly taken by them.* Today they are just one thing in front of Stella.

"Professor Dennis," a student shouts.

"What?" She's holding Rosie's dismembered hand.

"You were saying something about the muscle atrophy?"

"Yes." She's holding it as tight she can. "The muscles deteriorated over the course of two weeks, which is rapid for an ape."

"Chimp," someone shouts out.

"Chimps are apes. Just smarter smaller versions of the ones we see drinking beer in the commons." Everyone laughs, even the men, but as always, Noraki and Katuya don't laugh. They just take notes. On everything she says. She imagines that inside their composition books, along with exam dates, along with notes on the bone structure of prehistoric man, along with the charts and graphs that are inaccurate and unclear on the board, are the words she spoke a month ago about what she had for breakfast or what time she went to bed. The mundane things she said about Peter and John and Rosie—progress reports on her life, words that made her more human and less machine-like in front of them. They were sure to have scribbled notes that day she stopped mid-sentence and choked back what must've looked like a half-gallon of water. Inside that room, on that day, she felt as if she couldn't breathe, as if she were going to faint. It was the Wednesday before Thanksgiving break, the morning after she smelled sex inside Peter's mouth when he got home.

LOVE LIKE PRIMATES

"Go brush your teeth."

"Go fuck yourself."

Both of them were too tired from fighting to do what the other had asked.

Stella's sure that in Noraki and Katuya's notebooks, there exists some explanation, some historical sketch, that accounts for how she ended up here, holding this dead ape's hand—here, where all they can do is stare at her and all she can do is stare back. *The chimpanzees seem pleased just to see a human friend, one who demonstrates a level of interest or understanding for the chimp.*

"Show us her heart again," someone shouts from the back. As Stella reaches inside to pull it out, she is scared she may never let go of Rosie's hand.

Stella calls John when she gets home. She had four drinks and drove by the house fourteen times that she thinks Peter's fucking in. Like he's having an affair with the thing: the house, the windows, the doors. Or maybe the small manicured yard, the perfectly trimmed trees. This is exactly the type of house she would picture him fucking. The worst part (the dizzy from no sleep and 36 ounces of Whiskey Collins without the cherry part) is that Stella was in that house last spring. She was attending a Humanities faculty dinner party.

"Why'd they have it there?" John asks.

"The division chair was fucking her at the time."

"Did Peter know her then?"

"I introduced them."

"That stings."

Stella says nothing.

"Don't say 'nothing.' Whenever you say 'nothing', it's because you have a mouth full of something—what do you think?"

She thinks she's about to throw up all over the Ethan Allen Imitation Sofa from Ikea ($299); she thinks she's going to hang up the phone and call Peter, beg him to come back. "I think I'm going to die like Rosie."

"You need to stop working on that lecture."

"What was going on inside her head?" She gets up and makes herself another drink.

"You have to stop doing this."

"Why did Celeste hate me?" *The time in which a chimpanzee "lives" is limited to the past and the future.* Celeste had a baby. She told John it was his though things went downhill fast when timelines and calendar dates didn't match up.

"Oh, Christ."

John loved that baby—Michael—like it was his own. Still talks about him. Every now and then, he slips up and says things like: "my son," or, "our kid."

"I'm not going over this again with you."

"No. I don't mean the 'hate-me' part I know about. I mean before." *A chimpanzee's present would reveal more of the past if only the chimp were able to apply the plain after-effects of experience in its actions.*

"Before what?" He sounds tired and mad, like when they were kids, arguing over whose turn it was to clean the rabbits or feed the turtle.

"Before I told you it wasn't your kid."

"I think you need to get some sleep."

"I'm serious, John—I want to know."

"Oh fuck, I don't know." He sighs and the words coming through the phone sound heavy and lazy. "What do you want me to say? She thought you were judgmental and unforgiving. She thought that everything had to be your way. Even her relationship with me. Your terms. She said one time—" the pause warned it would be bad—"she told me one time that you can have any man you want, but that you'll never be able to keep him."

Stella pours club soda instead of whiskey. "And?"

"And that's why you choose to work with dead animals instead of the real ones with hearts and feelings."

"She said that about me?"

"Not so eloquently."

She shakes the ice in the glass. "Huh." And takes a sip. "I always thought she hated me because I was pretty." *As long as a chimpanzee's memory works only in this way, it may be an advantageous gift; it may also, however, be a real hindrance to the formation of valuable new behaviour.*

John tells her to get some sleep.

"I don't want to sleep."

"Stop working on the lecture. It won't solve anything."

"Did you ever tell Celeste that animals don't have feelings?"

"Good night, Stella."

In the morning, the whiskey bears down and locks her jaw into an unrelenting frown. "This isn't as much fun as it was when we were kids."

John packs up parts of Rosie, frozen and fractured, into what looks like a curbside trash bag. "What now?" she asks.

"Now, they just get rid of her." There are no classes today. The lab echoes resoundingly and the air is heavy with chemicals.

"Cremation?" She takes a handful of Advil.

"No. We need the bones."

"So, how do they…?"

"You don't want to know."

She swallows a handful. "You're right."

John makes a face and lifts Rosie's parts onto the university golf cart. Rosie is heavy, and John winces as he lifts. Pieces of her, however, are not as weighty as his face would indicate. Stella notices this. Then she notices *him*.

"Oh."

"Oh."

"Hi." Peter never did have good timing.

Stella doesn't look at him. She stares at the empty lab, which suddenly seems emptier, more sterile, more consumed by death and decay.

John gives Peter a "hey-man-even-though-I-sang-at-your-wedding-I've-been-telling-my-sister-to-leave-you-for-years" handshake, followed by the "we-are-like-family" pat on the shoulder, and, without looking back, gets in the golf cart and drives off, right out of the classroom like a funny little cartoon man—save for the chimp flopping around inside the Hefty bag.

"Key." Peter holds it up in his hand.

"Wow." He places it on the counter with a loud snap. "This is different," Stella says.

"Yeah."

She smiles and shakes her head.

"What?"

"For ten years, you've had a mouth on you like a fountain—a real conversationalist."

"Oh, Christ." Peter turns his back to her as she continues.

"At work, at parties, in the movies—people hushed you in-between bites of JuJu Bees." She paces, rearranging lab instruments. She's aware of the adrenaline that three sleepless nights can give you. "You talk on the phone for hours. You could put women in beauty shops to shame."

The clattering of scalpels and knives makes Peter nervous.

"And now, all you can say," Stella sputters, "Is 'yeah,' and, 'key!'"

"What're you doing?"

Apparently, what Stella is doing is holding a small scalpel in her hand and scaring the crap out of her husband who is leaving.

Peter motions with his eyes: Hand. Table. It's clear he's had some training handling women and sharp objects. Stella quickly puts the scalpel down, replacing it with a jar of Rosie's things instead. *When moving forms and objects, chimpanzees will start solving problems from a too-literal point of view; the chimpanzee will thus stop acting with the insight needed to succeed.* "So, what now?" She breathes slowly, moving glass containers of Rosie's blood and urine around the lab table.

"I've got a lawyer."

"Oh." She looks up. "I guess I should get a lawyer, too."

"This isn't funny, Stella."

"Was I laughing?"

Now he breathes slowly.

"What's all this?" He looks around the table and picks up a jar containing a slice of Rosie's liver.

"Parts of the chimp."

"Rosie?" He wrinkles his face in sadness, the lines deep with concern. Standing before her, Stella recognizes a man she hasn't seen in years. Someone decent—a man who liked canoeing and who used to sing old love songs to her. 'All of Me,' and 'Only You.'

"This is Rosie?"

She nods, letting loose the tears that have been locked up in some holding cell of her brain for the last several days—maybe even years.

"Hey." He puts the specimen down. "Are you going to be okay?"

He asks this, as if the answer would erase all the hurtful things said and done once love ceased being a reason for their staying together. As if it would erase every night Stella was unavailable and preoccupied, every waitress Peter fucked at his restaurant, every phone call he pretended was the wrong number, every time she let him pretend. As if it would make them forget every night he wasn't working late but instead was locked tightly between the thighs of a blonde, a brunette, a Sarah, an Amy—there was even a Xtava. ("She sounds like a Disney character. Like a mermaid, or a princess." "She's a beverage consultant." "She works at Starbucks.") Every last 'I love you,' 'fuck you,' and 'sorry I ever married you' would be solved—right here, right now. Everything he tried to be to her and everything she wouldn't let him be for all the reasons she never gave him the opportunity to understand. All would be put to rest with the one-word answer she would let float in the air, alongside Rosie's soul, above the array of pretty glass jars.

He grabs her hand.

Without thinking, without even stuttering, Stella says, "She slammed herself into the bars until she busted up her head so badly she bled to death." The jar shatters inside her hand and the glass goes in deep.

Peter pulls away.

"Flesh and skull and gray matter were all over the cage." Blood runs down her hands but she's not sure if it's hers or Rosie's because she can't feel anything. Not a damn thing. "It had to have taken at least six hours for her to bleed out that way."

"But I thought you said she died in…"

"I think we're both a little too tired for that now." She turns on the lab sink faucet and watches the red-stained water run off her fingers and down the drain.

Moments pass before she looks up, before anything is said. Just liquid swirling down the drain; they are both mesmerized by this display.

Peter is right there with a dry cloth. He covers the wound and puts his hand back over Stella's, stroking it softly. He strokes it and strokes it until it feels warm, the pain pure—until she realizes what he is in the process of giving back to her is much more than a key.

"Thank you," she says.

"Don't mention it," Peter says.

Stella slowly lets her hand slip from Peter's, and, for the first time in three days, only silence and space fill her mind.

There is a back way into the zoo. John and Stella found it when they were eleven and thirteen. Free. Up a hill, over a fence, and right into the ostrich cage *(Struthio camelus spatzi)*. Ostriches are mean and fast, and John and Stella both knew too much about them from a Mutual of Omaha special (and one episode of the A-Team) to try and outrun them. They would wait until about noon, when the birds would have to be moved into the cement cages because they couldn't take the western humidity and the California smog.

At 1:30 a.m. on a Tuesday, both Sala and Zeus (adopt a zoo animal and name it) are safely tucked away in their back suites, but Stella still hesitates.

Down Gorilla Lane and through the chimp exhibit, she hesitates to breathe. She tries to remember, as hard as she can, what it was like to be here when they were young. For those few hours, all of the animals, all their smells and sounds, would make everything okay. Just for a while. But now, with the moonlight hiding behind a synthetic tree, with Stella's hand still tingling and stinging, even the inside of this familiar space seems changed. Different, despite the chimps' snaps and whistles. Different for sure. For good.

Stella walks through the dark toward the bench where Rosie used to lie. She kicks the silver bowl that used to hold Rosie's yams and grains, and it goes spinning across the floor, all clean and sparkly.

Cedar Hill Books

DAUGHTER OF—*Kathleen Aguero*
$18—Poetry   ISBN: 1-891812-35-1

SET THIS BOOK ON FIRE!—*Jimmy Santiago Baca*
$15—Poetry   ISBN: 1-891812-23-8

THE HEAT: *Steelworker Lives and Legends*
$15—Prose & Poetry   ISBN: 1-891812-17-3

AMNESIA TANGO—*Alan Britt*
$10—Poetry   ISBN: 1-891812-14-9

AMERICAN MINOTAUR—*Leonard J. Cirino*
$9—Poetry   ISBN: 1-891812-22-X

96 SONNETS FACING CONVICTION—*Leonard J. Cirino*
$10—Poetry   ISBN: 1-891812-20-3

THE TERRIBLE WILDERNESS OF SELF—*Leonard J. Cirino*
$10—Poetry   ISBN:1-891812-00-9

THE JACKDAW POEMS—*Leonard J. Cirino*
$15—Poetry   ISBN:1-891812-32-7

the despairs—*Cid Corman*
$15—Poetry   ISBN: 1-891812-30-0

HANDFULS OF TIME—*Ruth Daigon*
$15—Poetry   ISBN: 1-891812-36-X

INFINITIES—*Lucille Lang Day*
$15—Poetry   ISBN: 1-891812-31-9

SUBURBAN LIGHT—*William Doreski*
$10—Poetry   ISBN: 1-891812-16-5

ANOTHER ICE AGE—*William Doreski*
$15—Poetry   ISBN: 1-891812-33-5

BODY AND SOUL—*Sharon Doubiago*
$15—Poetry   ISBN: 1-891812-24-6

THE SILK AT HER THROAT—*James Doyle*
$10—Poetry   ISBN: 1-891812-12-4

BLACK LIGHTNING—*Jean Flanagan*
$18—Poetry   ISBN: 1-891812-12-2

NEXT EXIT—*Taylor Graham*
$10—Poetry   ISBN: 1-891812-13-0

NORMAL ENOUGH—-*Yvette Hatrak*
$20—Fiction   ISBN: 1-891812-34-3

BEYOND RENEWAL—*George Held*
$10—Poetry   ISBN: 1-891812-29-7

WITHOUT PARADISE—*Richard Hoffman*
$15—Poetry ISBN: 1-891812-33-5

7th CIRCLE—*Maggie Jaffe*
$11—Poetry ISBN: 1-891812-07-6

THE PRISONS—*Maggie Jaffe*
$15—Poetry ISBN: 1-891812-21-1

SHADOW OF THE PLUM—*Carol Lem*
$15—Poetry ISBN: 1-891812-32-7

WHITHER AMERICAN POETRY—*Michael McIrvin*
$14—Critical Essays ISBN: 1-891812-26-2

THE BOOK OF ALLEGORY—*Michael McIrvin*
$10—Poetry ISBN:1-891812-03-3

OPTIMISM BLUES: Poems Selected & New—*Michael McIrvin*
$15—Poetry ISBN: 1-891812-37-8

PROVERBS FOR THE INITIATED—*Kenn Mitchell*
$11—Poetry ISBN: 1-891812-06-8

BRAMBLECROWN—*Georgette Perry*
$5—Poetry ISBN: 1-891812-25-4

GRAY AIR—*Christopher Presfield*
$8—Poetry ISBN: 1-891812-15-7

GUTTERSNIPE CANTICLE—*Amelia Raymond*
$9—Poetry ISBN: 1-891812-22-X

PARKING LOT MOOD SWING—*Doren Robbins*
$20—Poetry ISBN: 1-891812-11-4

"EDEN, OVER . . ."—*Tim Scannell*
$5—Poetry ISBN:1-891812-01-7

ROUTINE CONTAMINATIONS—*Deborah Small*
$24—Art / Prose ISBN: 1-891812-09-2

SOME SORT OF JOY—*John Taylor*
$15—Prose ISBN: 1-891812-08-4

THE WORLD AS IT IS—*John Taylor*
$15—Prose ISBN: 1-891812-04-1

KID WITH GRAY EYES—*Mark Terrill*
$10—Poetry ISBN: 1-891812-28-9

AMERIKA / AMERICA—*Marilyn Zuckerman*
$15—Poetry ISBN: 891812-40-8

PIECES OF EIGHT: *A Women's Anthology of Verse*
$10—Poetry ISBN: 1-891812-02-5

JAM: *Cedar Hill Anthology Series*
$10—Poetry ISBN: 1-891812-05-X